The Sound of Shiant

Hereward L.M. Proops

Cover Art by Chris Cowdrill www.chriscowdrill.co.uk

Copyright © 2011 by Hereward L.M. Proops

ISBN 978-1-4716-6754-1

First published in paperback in 2012

www.cruelharvest.blogspot.com

For Rebecca.

"Dh'iarr am muir a thadhal"

(the sea wants to be visited)

- old Gaelic proverb.

Prologue

13th February 1847

Lashed by the teeming rain, the deck of the Zarna was awash.

Captain Lorentzen barked an order at his men and watched as they set about lowering the foresail. Moving to the bow of the schooner and bracing a leg against the rail, he brought the telescope up to his eye and frantically searched the horizon for any sign of land. Darkness had fallen quicker than he had expected and the ferocity of the storm concerned him.

An experienced sailor, Lorentzen knew that the ship's best chance of surviving the storm would be to ride it out at sea and stay away from land. His concern was the possibility that the ship might be driven towards the nearby islands.

"I can't see them," he hollered. "What are they called again?"

"The Shiants," the mate replied. "They must be nearby."

"I hope not," Lorentzen roared over the howling wind. "I

don't think the mainsail can take much more of this!"

Lorentzen watched the mate move cautiously towards the stern of the ship. Without warning, a huge wave crashed against the side and knocked him off his feet. The telescope fell from his hands and was swept into the sea. Spluttering curses, Lorentzen hauled himself upright and followed the mate.

"This is madness," one of the men yelled to Lorentzen as he passed, "I've never seen anything like it."

"It will pass," Lorentzen reassured him, his own confidence shaken by the fall.

In the shelter of the cabin, the mate studied the charts laid out on the table before him.

"Well?" the captain burst into the cabin accompanied by the wailing of the storm. "Where are we?"

The mate looked up, his face ashen. "I... I don't know," he stammered.

Lorentzen leaned over the map and gave it a cursory examination. Though he had sailed the passage from Liverpool to Christianssund countless times, he knew the storm could well have blown them several miles off course. Without the stars to fix their position, the map was useless. A cry from the deck brought both the captain and the mate back outside.

"What is it?" Lorentzen called to the nearest sailor.

"There's a man in the water!" the sailor replied, pointing to the heaving waves.

Lorentzen and the mate quickly conducted a head count of the crew and both noted that all twelve men were onboard.

"All hands accounted for," Lorentzen shouted to the sailor.

"There can't be anyone in the waters!"

"I saw him," the terrified sailor answered. "Just to starboard."

Captain Lorentzen clung to the rail and checked the starboard side of the ship. The seething waters rose and fell, making it virtually impossible to see anything amidst the chaos of foam and spray.

"There's no one there now," he stated.

"Captain!" another sailor waved to him. "Over here! I saw a body!"

Hurrying over to the larboard side, Lorentzen joined a handful of sailors who gazed into the endlessly churning depths.

"I saw it," one man spoke, not moving his eyes from sea.

"It was a man," said another. "He looked straight at me."

"Are you sure?" Lorentzen asked. "The darkness plays tricks on your eyes."

"Captain," the first man dragged his gaze away from the waters to address him, "I know what I saw. There was a man there, I swear it."

Before Lorentzen could respond, a huge wave crashed into the ship. The Zarna lurched wildly to the side as the torrent of water cascaded over the deck. Terror stricken, the men hung onto the rail until the ship righted herself. Wiping salt water from his eyes, Lorentzen pulled himself to his feet and looked back out at the rolling sea.

"There," he called, pointing to a figure who flailed in the waters, "I see him!"

"It's young Julius!" the mate cried. "He was just swept over the side."

"Throw him a line," Lorentzen instructed. "We'll haul him back."

He watched as the rope was tossed out to the floundering man. Julius grabbed hold of it and the men at the other end began to pull. The storm continued to rage all around them and the icy rain began to sting Lorentzen's cheeks.

Julius yelled something but the roaring wind and the crashing waves smothered the sound.

"What's that he says?" the mate asked.

"He says to pull harder," a sailor responded.

The man in the water yelled again, his cries growing more vociferous.

"Pull harder," Lorentzen ordered. "You need to pull harder."

"No!" the mate shouted. "He says that something is pulling him."

"We're pulling him," one of the sailors answered as he hauled on the rope.

Lorentzen peered into the darkness at the struggling figure that clung to the end of the line. Three strong men hauled on the rope but seemed to be having little success bringing Julius back to the ship. The young sailor cried out again and sank beneath the waves. The men holding the rope fell backwards as the weight on the other end suddenly vanished.

"Julius!" the mate shrieked, leaning over the railing with a lantern in his hand.

"He's gone," Lorentzen groaned. "We've got to save the ship. Turn her about!"

"Come about!" roared the mate.

The helmsman turned the ship's wheel and the boom of the mainsail swung over the deck as it caught the wind. Most of the crew had heard the mate's call and so ducked but one unlucky fellow was struck with the full force of the boom. Lorentzen watched in horror as the man was thrown into the water.

"Man overboard!" he yelled.

The ship swung about as she tacked and by the time the crew were able to respond to Lorentzen's cry the body was nowhere to be seen. The mate staggered over to his side and pointed towards an indistinct dark mass that rose out of the gloom before them.

"Over there," he bellowed. "There's land. It must be the Shiants!"

"We'll have to sail against the wind if we want to stay off those rocks," Lorentzen stated. "Trim the sail!"

The men hauled on the lines to bring the sail in. The canvas was stretched taut as the men fastened the lines to the cleats. The ship ploughed on in the face of the wind. For a time, it seemed that she was making progress, but the strain on the lines proved too much.

One by one, the cleats snapped and the sail, free from its bindings, took the full brunt of the storm. A jagged tear appeared in the canvas and the torn sail began to flap wildly in the wind. A sharp crack told the crew that the mast had broken and they covered their heads as it crashed to the deck.

"Faen!" the mate swore. "What now, Captain?"

Lorentzen did not answer, his attention focused on the swirling waters. Something grey and sleek had surfaced momentarily before slipping back into the depths. He rubbed his eyes as the mate grasped him by the arm.

"Captain!" the mate implored. "What should we do?"

Shaking his head, Lorentzen pushed past the mate and examined the mast. There was no chance of repairing it in the storm and without it the ship was drifting helplessly. The remaining sailors stared at him, waiting for orders. Lorentzen's head swam as he looked at the devastation on deck. His hands shook as he reached for the cross he wore around his neck.

Fear spread quickly amongst the men. Some began to pray whilst others fastened themselves to the ship with rope. A few ran to the side of the ship and bawled pleas for help into the darkness. Lorentzen pulled his cap down tighter on his head and stepped over the fallen mast before moving to the stern of the ship. Turning his back on the crew, his eyes searched the dark horizon for any sign of respite from the storm.

"Tha breac an rionnaich air an adhar..." a voice was carried on the wind.

"Who is that?" Lorentzen called in response.

He leaned over the rail and looked at the billowing waves. Beneath them darted the strange grey shape he had seen before.

"There's something here!" he exclaimed. "It's in the water!"

His calls went unanswered as the ship turned in the storm. Without the sail, she was defenceless against combined force of the wind and the tide. The men clung to whatever was to hand as she was spun and tossed by the squall. The waves broke over the sides and swept whatever was not tied down into the tumultuous waters. The wind lifted any ropes hanging loose and whipped them in the air.

One lashed the mate on the side of his face, the swipe leaving him bloodied and bewildered. He lurched towards Lorentzen and pointed to the starboard side where a band of white surf could be seen in the darkness.

"Breakers, Captain!" he screamed. "She's going to run right into them."

The timbers of the ship cried out as she was thrown against the rocks. The starboard side crumpled and splintered with the impact. The deck beneath the sailors' feet ruptured, the planks bowing and splitting as they were wrenched from their housing. Lorentzen looked down with horror at the foaming white waters beneath the ship.

"Stay on board!" he shrieked to his crew. "There's something in the water!"

"I see them!" the mate whimpered. "Dozens of them. They're swimming round us!"

The ship listed as another wave crashed into her side, pounding her onto the rocks. Thrown off balance by the impact, the mate plummeted over the side. The groan of breaking wood and the roar of rushing water smothered his cries for help as he floundered in the surging waves. The mate struggled to keep his head above water and Lorentzen quickly lost sight of him.

Broken by the rocks, the Zarna began to take on water. Knowing the ship was doomed, the sailors began jumping overboard and clinging to any ballast they could find. Resolving to go down with his ship, Lorentzen hung onto the ruins of the stern. He watched with dread as the grey shapes circled those who bobbed in the water. Seeing the strange forms surrounding them, the men cried out with terror and began paddling back towards the remains of the ship. One by one, the men disappeared, dragged beneath the surface by unseen hands.

Scrambling to find purchase on the slick remnants of the deck, Lorentzen uttered a prayer. The freezing rain continued to pelt him and he shivered as he huddled beside the ruined stump of the main mast. The cries from the water had ceased and only the chattering of his teeth competed with the sounds of the storm. There was a tremendous crash and the stern broke off from the rest of the wreck. Lorentzen plummeted into the cold waters and went under. Fighting his way to the surface, he gasped for breath and treaded water as he got his bearings. With the loss of the stern, there was nothing to prevent the rest of the ship breaking up. The sea was littered with floating debris and Lorentzen watched despondently as the larger pieces of the schooner slipped beneath the waves.

Caught by the ferocious current, Lorentzen found himself drawing near to the white foam where the waves broke against the rocks. Knowing that it would be futile to fight against the tide, he swam towards the breakers. Lifted by a huge wave, Lorentzen was slammed onto the rocks. The wind knocked out of his lungs, he desperately clung to the slick black rock, squeezing his fingertips into the cracks along its surface. Wave after wave mercilessly battered him but he held on, sobbing with each breath he was able to draw.

Exhausted by the relentless fury of the storm, Lorentzen's grip on the rock began to weaken. As his legs slipped into the water he felt a hand clamp around his ankle. The grip was strong and a sharp tug further loosened Lorentzen's hold. He clawed desperately at the slippery surface but was gradually pulled further and further into the water. His bleeding fingers slithered out of the cracks and Lorentzen felt a cold arm wrap itself around his neck.

"Latha math a-màireach," the creature whispered in his ear before it dragged him beneath the waves.

Chapter 1

April 1882

The deep waters of the Sound of Mull were calm. For that, Inspector Edmund Forrester decided, he should be thankful.

Though a strong swimmer, Forrester hated travelling by steamship much as he hated travelling by hansom cab, steam train or any other form of transport he was not in direct control of.

Clinging to the railing, Forrester watched the miles of water splash by as the SS Claymore steamed on to her destination. Brought into service only the previous year, the ship was spotless. The clean white paint covering the superstructure appeared bright in the morning sunshine in contrast to the black paintwork of the hull. The funnel that topped the ship bore the unmistakeable black and red colouring of the MacBrayne fleet and a steady stream of smoke billowed from it and drifted off into the clear April skies.

They had left Glasgow at two o'clock the previous afternoon. The journey down the Firth of Clyde had been uneventful enough but lack of sleep had left Forrester feeling groggy. The steady drone of the engines accompanied by the vociferous snoring of the travelling companion with whom he shared the cabin had kept him awake until the early hours. He had slept fitfully for a few hours before the ship's horn announced their arrival at Oban just before eight o'clock that morning.

The wind whipped through his hair as a light sea spray blew into his face. He wiped the moisture from his thick moustache and made a futile effort to bring some order to his ruffled hair. Muttering a curse, he dug in his pocket for his cigarette case. Extracting one, he patted the numerous pockets of his greatcoat in search of his matches.

"Gie ye help wi' tha'?" a voice spoke with a broad Glaswegian accent.

Forrester looked up at the young man dressed in the steward's uniform who sheltered a lit match in his hands. The man's shaggy blond hair was ruffled by the steady breeze and a broad, genial smile seemed permanently set on his youthful features.

Accepting the light, Forrester thanked the man and turned his attentions back to the waters.

"It's no' bad the now, but I'll wager it'll be grim once we reach the Minch," the steward commented as he flicked the match over the side.

Forrester nodded, his gaze remaining fixed on the foaming wake of the ship. Seemingly ignorant of Forrester's desire to remain undisturbed, the steward continued to prattle on.

"Tha's Lismore," he pointed to the island growing smaller behind the ship. "Over there, tha's Craignure. We'll be stoppin' by there shortly. My brother works the port."

Forrester gave a noncommittal grunt and hoped the man

would leave him alone.

"Prize-fighter, are ye?" the steward asked, his eyes fixed on Forrester's flattened nose.

Forrester shook his head solemnly, his hands clenching the railing before him. Though he had been asked the same question countless times it never failed to anger him. His nose had been broken during an attempt to apprehend a criminal a dozen years ago. It wasn't just his good looks that had suffered that fateful night. His failure to catch the felon had also damaged his pride. His inability to cope with the situation had distanced him from Lillian. When she left, all that remained was his work.

"My brother- no' the one in Craignure but the one who lives in Govan - he does a spot o'fightin' now an' then," the steward continued, seemingly ignorant of Forrester's growing irritation. "Mebbe when y'passin' this way again I could arrange a meet..."

"I'm a police inspector," Forrester muttered.

"English are ye?" the younger man balked. "Och, I didnae ken the first. Where ye headed?"

"Stornoway."

"Stornoway!" he chuckled. "What business have ye goin' all the way there?"

"A family matter," Forrester answered vaguely. Sensing that his reticence was not going to deter the young man, Forrester decided to put his garrulousness to good use. He opened his cigarette case and offered it to the man.

"Have you been working the ships a long time?"

"No' long," the man smiled as he placed a cigarette in his mouth and helped himself to another for behind his ear. "Chust a few month."

"The Claymore does this trip often, does she not?"

"Aye, every Thursday she sails. Rain or shine," the steward smiled. "Tends to be rain this time o' year."

"You've seen bad weather then?"

"Bad?" the steward spat over the side, "The worst. The devil hisself could no' conjure worse than the Minch on a bad day."

"And the Long Island?" Forrester asked, referring to his destination, "How is it up there?"

"Fair enough," the steward sniffed, "Once ye get past the Minch. The Islanders, they're a sturdy breed. Tougher than mos' Hielan'."

"High-lan?" Forrester asked.

"Aye," the young man smiled, "Hielan'. High-land-ers... y'ken? Aye well, they're no' such a bad lot. Mad about fish."

"Fish?"

"Aye, fish. Ye'll see herring everywhere in Stornoway. In summer ye cannae see the Minch for boats. No' so many go out in winter, but there's still plenty trade."

The steward sucked noisily on his cigarette before throwing it over the side. Wishing Forrester luck on his travels, he stepped back inside the ship. Forrester remained on deck to consider the events of the past week.

***

It had not been the letter from Lillian that had surprised him. His ex-wife had written several short, curt notes to him since their divorce. The first came a year after the divorce had been made official and she told him that she planned to move to Scotland. The second had arrived a few months after that and had informed him that she was engaged to a Mister Boyd McCormick. A silence of nine years had followed during which time Forrester assumed that Lillian had forgotten his existence. Two months ago, he had received another letter accompanied by an invitation to her wedding in Glasgow.

In the letter Lillian had sent her best wishes to him and apologised for her lack of contact over the years, though gave no explanation for her silence. Such vagueness came as no surprise to Forrester, who was familiar with his ex-wife's temperament. The invitation to her wedding, however, had surprised him. He had assumed that his wife would have tied the knot during the nine years of silence and would by now have given Mister Boyd McCormick numerous children. Most surprising was the fact that his ex-wife wished him to be present at the ceremony. Reluctantly, he had accepted the invitation. If Lillian had been good-natured enough to invite the man who broke her heart, the least he could do would be to attend. He had spoken to the Chief Inspector and, being owed substantial holiday time, had arranged a couple of weeks off work.

The wedding itself had been a typically sombre Scottish affair. The weather had been grey and overcast and the ceremony had been conducted by a scowling priest who joylessly united the couple.

The reception was no more cheerful. The guests of the bride huddled around Lillian, cooing over her dress. The guests of the groom crowded around the bar and drank themselves into a stupor. Forrester, already feeling awkward as the bride's ex-husband, found himself sat next to the groom's brother.

Colin McCormick was a boisterous young man who ate and drank without restraint and regaled the table with crude, tuneless drinking songs. Having endured this most disagreeable wedding breakfast, Forrester had planned to excuse himself and return to his hotel room. He wondered what had drawn him here in the first place, but quickly remembered when he saw Lillian.

She looked radiant, her long white dress accentuating the blush of rouge on her cheeks. She wore her hair in plaits, much as she had on their wedding day, and the sight of her smiling and laughing with her cousins turned his stomach. Forrester drained his whisky and, picking up his hat, made a move towards the door. Spotting his attempt the leave, Lillian disengaged herself from her entourage and hurried over to him.

"Oh, Eddie!" she chided, "You're not leaving already are you?"

"I don't think it's really appropriate for me to stay any longer, is it?"

"Nonsense!" she laughed, placing her hand on his arm and leading him back into the room, "I want you here. I want you to be happy for me."

"I am," he lied, "I'm very happy for you."

She looked into his eyes. "And you, Edmund... Are you happy?"

"Lily," he sighed and placed his hand on hers, "you know me. My work keeps me happy."

She gazed at him as though trying to weigh the truth in his words, then took him by the hand and led him over to the bar.

"You simply must meet Boyd's cousin, Calum," she said.

"I've told him all about you."

Calum Mackinnon grasped Forrester's hand in a bone-crushing grip and smiled through his heavy red beard.

"Lullian's told much about ye," he beamed. "It's no' all good mind!"

"Calum, you rotter!" Lillian screeched and playfully slapped his broad chest. "I'll leave you two to get acquainted."

"Lullian tells us ye're wi' the polis," Mackinnon began. "Why are ye no' in uniform?"

"I'm with the Criminal Investigation Department," Forrester said, helping himself to a glass of whisky from the bar. "I don't wear a uniform."

"Aye well, she said ye was all work and nae play," Mackinnon chuckled. "I didnae believe her but I sees it now. Dinnae get me wrong. I didnae wish to offend ye, it's chust that I have a wee problem of my own. I think ye might be the man to help."

"Glasgow isn't my jurisdiction," Forrester said with a dismissive wave of his hand.

"That's chust as well," Mackinnon continued, "I'm no' talkin' about Glasgow. I'm from Lewis, ye ken?"

"Lewes? I've been to the South Downs but never to-"

"Not Lewes!" Mackinnon interrupted. "The Isle of Lewis. Leòdhas... In the Hebrides, man."

"Oh," Forrester mumbled, "I've never been that far North."

"Few have," Mackinnon smiled. "But it's gey fair. Perhaps ye'd pay us a visit? Ye could help us wi' our wee problem."

"Does Lewis not have its own police force?"

"Oh aye, there is that, but they're no help. To a man they're in the pocket of Murdo Macleod, an' he's the problem."

Forrester sipped his whisky and held the fiery spirit in his mouth for a moment. The news of corruption in the police did not shock him. It had not been five years since three high ranking detectives of his acquaintance had been tried for corruption at the Old Bailey. Although many forces had begun to clean up their acts since the trial, he could see how a small rural police force would be able to continue such bad practices without attracting the attention of the authorities on the mainland.

"How do you think I could be of use?" he asked.

"Our Boyd's tellin' us how Lullian left ye 'cause ye wouldnae let a case go. Sounds to me ye're chust the kind o' man I need."

"And why is that?" Forrester snarled, his patience running thin.

"They killed my son," Mackinnon answered.

***

Forrester filled his lungs with the clean sea air. He leaned against the rail and watched the blue flag with intertwined red and blue crosses of the MacBrayne fleet flap in the breeze. He scowled as he thought of Mackinnon's plea. That was why he had been invited to Lillian's wedding. She had not really wanted him there; it had all been set up in order for him to meet Boyd's cousin and listen to the tale of his missing child.

It certainly was an intriguing story. Having had a fancy for the sea since a young age, young Alistair Mackinnon had been working on Murdo Macleod's fishing boat for a few weeks. Being the youngest member of the crew, he was given the most menial tasks but he took his job seriously and was keen to learn as much as possible, it being his dream to one day own a fishing boat of his own. In September, Macleod's boat had left Stornoway in calm weather and headed for the fishing grounds to the south of the island. According to Macleod's account, a storm had blown in from the south-west and taken the fishermen unawares. The small boat had been tossed around violently and Alistair had fallen overboard and had been taken by the undercurrent.

Calum Mackinnon, however, believed that Macleod and his men had thrown his son overboard in an effort to lighten the boat. He had appealed to both the police and the magistrates of the islands but his claims had been dismissed as fantasies brought on by the grief of losing his only son. Forrester would have been inclined to believe the magistrates but there was something in Calum Mackinnon's eyes that had convinced him. Forrester trusted his instincts, they rarely let him down. By following his hunches, Forrester had managed to close several cases that had been thought to be unsolvable. Some fellow officers said he had "a nose for crime", though never to his face.

Why had he agreed to travel to the Island and investigate the story of the missing child? It certainly was not within his jurisdiction and he had no business getting involved in such a case. He had told the steward that it was a family matter but he was aware that such a claim was tenuous to say the least.

His ex-wife's husband's cousin could hardly be called a member of his family. What other reason did he have for going? He had the time to go. According to the records, he had not taken a holiday for over ten years. Chief Inspector Pardoe had willingly granted Forrester a leave of absence to attend the wedding and he had sent a brief note requesting an additional week's absence. Deep in his heart, Forrester knew this was not a holiday. He was working, just as he would be had he ignored Lillian's invitation.

The ship steamed on, past the craggy, gnarled cliffs of the Scottish west coast. As they moved into deeper waters, the waves became noticeably larger and Forrester clung tighter to the railing as he felt the deck pitch beneath his feet.

"Ye'll get used tae it soon enough," a voice spoke behind him.

"Hello, Colin," Forrester sighed, wishing his travelling companion had remained inside. The boisterous young man swaggered over to his side and slouched over the rail. He was in his early twenties and full of the flawed confidence of his age. Colin wore the latest fashions and had allowed his hair to grow long, longer than Forrester deemed suitable for a gentleman. He was loud, ill-mannered and had the unnerving habit of winking when he spoke.

"Calum tells me ye've no' seen the islands before."

"That's correct. Do you visit much?"

"Och, no!" the young man exclaimed. "The last time I was there was Calum an' Maggie's wedding. I was nae older than wee Alistair. I'm a city man, I'm no' comfortable in the Hielan'."

"Why did you agree to come then?" Forrester probed.

"Calum didnae want ye travellin' alone," Colin grinned, "seein' ye dinnae have the Gaelic."

"And do they not speak English on the islands?"

"Some do," Colin scratched his head. "Some do, but likely they'd act as though they couldnae to a Sassenach as yersel'."

"So they are hostile to the English?"

"Hostel?" Colin chuckled and shook his head. "Gracious no. Distrustin' mebbe, but no' hostel. Ye must be mindful that they dinnae have much to dae wi' the English, 'cept maybe sellin' fish."

"Are you fluent in Gaelic?"

Colin blushed. "No' floo-went. As I said, I'm no' so Hielan' as Calum an' his kin. I ken it well, mind. My ma was from the islands."

Forrester nodded and turned his attention back to the deep blue waters. The waves were bigger now and sprayed the deck as they crashed against the side of the ship. Many of the other passengers had retreated from the deck to the comfortable interior and Forrester contemplated retiring to his own cabin.

"The steward said the waters would get worse when we reached the Minch," Forrester commented. "It seems he was correct."

"Och, yes," Colin smirked. "The Minch is cruel, cruel waters. But this is no' the Minch. We're no' even past Eigg yet. Ye'll know tomorro' when we're in the Minch."

Colin McCormick's prediction was right. The next afternoon, as the ship rose and fell and the stinging rain lashed against the side of his face, Forrester knew that the Claymore had reached the notorious stretch of water. He retched drily over the rail, having nothing in his stomach left to vomit. Gasping, he straightened himself and wiped his mouth on his sleeve. The rain came down in heavy grey sheets that prevented seeing anything further than a dozen yards to either side of the ship. Land had been in sight for most of the journey and now, surrounded by churning waters and dark clouds, Forrester felt a pang of terror.

Colin seemed unaffected by the storm. Occasionally, he detached himself from the warmth of their cabin to check that Forrester had not fallen overboard but never stayed for long. Though nauseous and shivering with cold, Forrester was glad to be left alone, hating to be seen by anyone in such a weakened condition. He spat and staggered weakly over to a bench where he collapsed and hung his head between his knees.

Lillian. In such moments of weakness, his mind always went back to Lillian. She was the reason he had agreed to this ridiculous journey. What did he hope to achieve with such an undertaking? Would solving the mystery of Alistair Mackinnon's fate bring her back to him? Deep down, he knew that it would not. His one chance at happiness had passed. Lillian was gone; her heart belonged to another man. Forrester groaned and clung to his seat as the ship steamed further on into the storm.

Chapter 2

Stornoway was not at all what Forrester had expected. Stepping off the ship he found himself overwhelmed by the noise and activity on the waterfront. Dozens of small vessels bobbed alongside the bulk of the Claymore, their naked masts pointing into the sky. Even more boats were run aground on a gently shelving beach that stretched up to the esplanade.

Although the fishing season had not yet begun in earnest there were hordes of fishermen loitering on the quayside. Having unloaded their catch into vast wooden troughs, they leaned against the walls and watched the army of herring girls sort, gut and pack the fish into barrels. Vast nets dripping with seawater were hung out to dry next to the boats. Children idly picked the trails of seaweed that clung to the nets and watched their fathers chat and laugh and smoke with their fellow sailors. The smell of the nearby smokehouses where the fish were cured lingered in the air and made Forrester's mouth water.

Clutching his carpetbag, Forrester followed Colin McCormick as he threaded his way through the crowds.

"That was South Beach," Colin called over his shoulder, "North Beach is chust up ahead. It's no' different tae South Beach, 'cept it faces North. In the summer months ye cannae move for fish."

"Where are we going?" Forrester looked around, eager to get his bearings in the strange new town.

"Cromwell Street," Colin answered. "We'll get ye a room there. I'll be stayin' at Calum's but we reckoned ye'd be gey comfortable at the Royal."

"The Royal?" Forrester asked. "Is that a hotel?"

"That it is," Colin replied. "It's no' cheap but it's better than sharin' the floor wi' me."

Colin led Forrester through numerous narrow cobbled streets. The young man walked briskly, occasionally glancing round to check that Forrester was keeping up with his pace. As they walked, Forrester heard strains of Gaelic drifting from doorways and open windows. Passing a particularly heated exchange emanating from an open window, he cocked his head to listen to the unfamiliar tongue.

"D'ye ken what they're sayin'?" Colin asked.

"Not a word," Forrester admitted. "It's quite unlike anything I've ever heard before."

"Aye, that's right," the young man laughed. "It's a devil of a tongue to understand if ye havnae heard it afore."

"What are they saying?" Forrester wondered aloud.

"Och, they're chust talkin' about the weather," Colin answered, having listened to the exchange for a moment.

"But they sound so angry..."

"Everythin' sounds angry that ye cannae make sense o'!"

Colin shrugged. "I ken this Russian lad. Lived in the Gorbals next tae a chum o'mine. Couldnae understand a word he said. To hear him speak ye'd've thought he was fixin' tae kill ye, but he was as nice as anythin' if ye bought him a dram."

They continued on until they came onto a broader, busier thoroughfare. Horse-drawn carts clattered by on the cobbles and the gaudy shop-fronts advertised the same wares as could be seen in any high street shop.

"Cromwell Street," Colin informed him. "The Royal's no' much further."

The street followed the edge of the bay and all the way along its length Forrester could see the masts of boats and the gatherings of herring girls. Like at South Beach, huge numbers of barrels were stacked along the shoreline.

"Herring," Colin commented. "In the summer months they land tens o' thousands o' barrels worth. It's good trade but ye cannae find lodgings in season. Folks from all over drift in tae Stornoway tae work."

The Royal Hotel was a large, whitewashed building that sat overlooking the bay. Across the water lay the young woodland which surrounded the imposing bulk of Lews castle, the vast country residence built by the recently deceased Sir James Matheson. Forrester followed Colin into the reception where an elderly man with a whisper of grey hair on his otherwise bald head took his bags.

"Ciamar a tha sibh?" he smiled toothlessly.

"He's askin' if ye're well," Colin whispered. "Many o' the older folks dinnae speak English."

"Tell him I'm very well, thank you," Forrester answered. "And ask him if I can have a room for the week."

Colin and the old man exchanged words in the strange tongue whilst Forrester listened. He heard his own name several times, along with 'Detective Inspector' so he assumed that Colin was regaling the old man with his reasons for being there. The rest was completely alien, a rhythmical series of lilting sounds that bore no resemblance to any other language he was familiar with. Uncomfortable with being the subject of conversation, Forrester stood by the window and watched the small boats paddle around the still waters of the bay. The old man laughed out loud and reached for a key hanging behind the desk.

"They've got a room for ye," Colin said. "Angus here'll show ye. If ye dinnae mind, I'll be headin' tae Calum's now. I'll be back for ye on Monday."

"Monday?" Forrester asked. "I'd prefer to start looking into the matter tomorrow."

"On the Sabbath?" Colin snorted with laughter. "Ye'll find there's no' much goin' on tomorro', Inspector. They're very observant of the Sabbath on the islands and they dinnae like any kind of disruption to their worship, you ken? Ye'd be best off makin' a start on Monday."

"Very well," Forrester sighed and extended a hand. "I'll be seeing you Monday morning."

Colin shook his hand and swaggered out of the hotel. The old man looked at Forrester expectantly.

"A bheil Gàidhlig agaibh?" he asked.

"I'm afraid I don't understand," Forrester grinned awkwardly.

"Dè thuirt thu?" the man frowned.

"I don't understand," Forrester repeated, raising his voice a little louder.

The old man groaned as he picked up the carpet bag and signalled that Forrester should follow him. He led him up two flights of stairs to the upper floor. After unlocking a door, the old man pushed it open and indicated that Forrester should enter. The door-frame was low and Forrester had to stoop as he stepped into the room. It was plainly decorated; a single bed was pushed up beneath a small window, a dresser up against another wall. A Celtic cross hanging on the wall was the only ornamentation to be seen. The old man deposited Forrester's bag on the floor and raised his eyebrows.

"A bheil an t-acras ort?" he asked as he mimed the motion of eating.

"No," Forrester shook his head. "No, thank you."

"Ceart gu leòr," the man shrugged and excused himself, leaving Forrester alone in the room.

The ageing springs creaked loudly as Forrester sat down on the bed. The bedsheets were clean and stiff with starch, the pillows firm and unyielding. A light rain began to patter on the windowpane and he pulled off his coat and loosened his tie.

Tossing the heavy pillows onto the floor, he folded his greatcoat beneath his head and lay back. He closed his eyes and took a deep breath. Though tired and sickened by the journey, sleep would not come easily. Every time he cleared his mind, Lillian came skipping over to him in her wedding dress and took him by the hand.

***

He woke with a start. Disorientated by the strange

surroundings, he stumbled from the bed and gazed out of the window. It was still dark outside but the gentle glow of dawn was beginning to creep over the horizon. The light streaming from his window glistened on the black waters of the bay. The streets seemed empty and the hotel curiously quiet. He checked his pocket-watch and saw that it read half past six. He had expected that there would be some sign of life at this time in the morning but the town appeared to be deserted.

Having splashed some cold water on his face Forrester straightened his clothes and ran a comb through his unruly hair. Satisfied that it was not obvious that he had slept fully clothed, he stepped out into the hallway in search of breakfast.

The hotel was silent. No voices could be heard through the doors and as he walked downstairs he was conscious of the fact that the curtains remained drawn and the fireplaces untended.

"Hello?"

His call brought no response. He shivered as he moved into the lounge. He drew back the curtains to allow the cold morning light into the room. Leather armchairs crowded around a stone hearth. A carriage clock resting on the mantelpiece quietly counted the seconds. Empty glasses littered the tables and the smell of stale smoke emanated from the ornate ashtrays standing between chairs. Wishing he had worn his coat, Forrester knelt by the fire and tried to stir the embers back to life. He added the contents of coal scuttle and began to blow on the glowing cinders.

"Ye shouldnae be doin' that!" a voice screeched.

Startled, he spun around and saw a plump woman standing in the doorway. Her arms were folded across her substantial bosom and she glared disapprovingly at him.

"It's no' your place tae be lightin' fires," she scolded. "I take it ye're the Englishman stayin' wi'us?"

Forrester nodded, noting the curl of the woman's lip as she spoke the word "Englishman".

"Well I'm sure ye didnae mean any harm," she continued, throwing a cup of water to douse the flames growing in the hearth, "but we tend no' to light a fire until after church."

"I'm sorry, I didn't realise," he muttered. "There was nobody around and I thought-"

"Och, there were people around," she interjected. "Listenin' to ye stomp around an' yellin' at the top o' yer lungs. Sunday's a day o' rest on this island, d'ye ken?"

Realising it was futile to continue any further, Forrester decided to change the topic of conversation.

"Would it be possible for me to have some breakfast?" he asked.

"Breakfast?" she tutted. "I'll fetch ye some bread an' butter but I'm no' goin' tae cook for ye on the Sabbath."

She returned a moment later with a plate of buttered bread and a small hunk of cheese. Forrester thanked her and devoured the food hungrily. After eating he returned to his room to fetch his overcoat before stepping out to explore the town.

The morning was chilly and grey. A light rain fell and Forrester felt the dull ache of the cold breeze on his exposed skin. Cursing the Scottish weather, he buttoned up the coat and stuffed his hands into his pockets. He walked back down Cromwell Street in the direction of the town, admiring the neatness and tidiness of the streets. The town was deserted. There were no pedestrians browsing the shop windows, no horses and carts clattering down the cobbled roads. A blanket of silence covered the small town, only broken by the sound of his footsteps echoing in the empty streets. Retracing his steps from the previous day, he soon found himself standing at the esplanade of North Beach. The crowds, the noise and the activity of Saturday afternoon had all vanished. All that remained were the lingering smells of smoked fish and seaweed.

He walked between the countless stacks of barrels, amazed that so much fish could be taken from the sea and marvelling at how the industry was supported by the work of the whole community.

The huge wooden troughs, around which he had seen the herring girls stood, were empty, piles of wicker baskets piled high next to them. The smaller boats rested on the beach, their lines tapping against the masts in the breeze. The larger boats were anchored out in the shallows, gently bobbing on the tide. Forrester sat on a barrel and watched the waves idly lap at the shore. It was clear that Colin McCormick had been right; there would be no chance of speaking to the fishermen today.

A voice disturbed his reverie. "Dè tha thu a dèanamh?"

Forrester looked up from the waves into the dark brown eyes of a young woman. She was tall and slender, her head covered by a tattered scarf that did not stop a strand of dark hair from falling in front of her eyes.

"I'm sorry," he smiled, "I don't understand."

"What are ye doin' here?"

"Just looking," he replied.

"There's nothin' tae look at," she giggled. "There's no-one here."

"I was just getting acquainted with the town," Forrester

said, glancing around. "It's very peaceful here."

"What d'ye expect on a Sunday?"

"I'd have thought it would be quiet," he reflected, striking a match off the side of the barrel and holding the flame to the cigarette hanging from his lips, "but this is quite something else. Where is everybody?"

"Where d'ye think?" she frowned. "They're all preparin' for church. Give us a bit o' that."

Forrester handed her the cigarette and watched as she puffed away contentedly on it.

"I'm Effie Morrison."

"Edmund Forrester." He held out his hand.

"English are ye?" Effie stared at the proffered hand but did not reach for it.

"Yes, I am," he answered. "I'm here on business."

"What kind o' business?"

"I'm looking for someone. Do you know Murdo Macleod?"

"I know several Murdo Macleods. I'll wager ye'll be lookin' for the fisherman Murdo Macleod."

"You know the man?"

"Och, everyone knows him." She turned and pointed to a large twin-masted boat that was anchored in the water. "That's one of his boats, the Manannán. He claims it tae be the fastest in all the islands."

"Does he own many boats?" Forrester asked.

"Four or five, I reckon. But that's his biggest." Effie tossed the end of the cigarette aside. "A fair few o' the lads work for him."

"And you? Do you work for him?"

"Away wi' ye," she laughed, "I'd sooner lay an egg than be let in a herrin' boat. It's bad luck tae let a woman aboard. Us gyurls work for Boabie Nicolson, the cooper."

Forrester walked to the edge of the water in order to get a better look at the boat. The main mast was huge, reaching nearly seventy feet into the sky. Unlike many of the other boats, the Manannán had a deck to provide shelter for the crew in a storm. The name was emblazoned on the side of the vessel in an ornate script which stood out against the bright red paintwork. The sails were neatly stowed away and the tidy coils of ropes on the deck gave him the impression that this was a boat that was well looked after.

"What can you tell me about Macleod?" he asked.

"He's rich," she said, pushing a pebble into the wet sand with her boot. "Strict, too. Runs his boats like the navy. Most men are too scared tae question him."

"I see," Forrester responded, quickly forming an opinion of the man.

The young woman pushed the unruly strand of hair away from her eyes and smiled.

"I must be goin'. It's been nice to meet you, Edmund Forrester."

"And you too, Miss Morrison," he said. "I hope we'll meet again."

"I daresay," she called over her shoulder as she walked away. "The island's no' big."

Forrester spent the next hour wandering the deserted

streets. The town was small but the displays in the shop windows and the modern gas lighting showed signs of prosperity. Just before ten o'clock the streets suddenly filled with people, all in their Sunday best. The women wore plain skirts and blouses, their hair covered by hats or scarves similar to that worn by Effie Morrison. The men dressed in dark suits of an austere cut. The townspeople walked in reverential silence through the town. Having nothing better to do, Forrester resolved to follow them.

The Free English Church stood on the corner of Francis Street and Kenneth Street. A solid, modern construction, the building seemed well suited to its orderly surroundings. Still following the crowd, Forrester entered the church and took a seat to the rear of the congregation. Although he had been a regular churchgoer in previous years, he had stopped attending since his divorce, feeling that he was somewhat unworthy of sharing in such fellowship. He sat and listened to the whole service but did not derive any kind of comfort or pleasure from it. The words that had once seemed so significant and relevant to his life now seemed meaningless.

The church Mr and Mrs Forrester had attended together was the same one in which they had been wed. It was small and poor and in the winter was uncomfortably cold. The vicar was a frail old man whose voice was so quiet that one had to strain to hear him clearly. However, the congregation knew one another well and the services were always well attended. Forrester smiled as he fondly recalled the sensation of Lillian pressed against him in the crowded pews. Sometimes he would listen to the sermons and feel inspired by them. Other times he would sit with nothing more on his mind than the Sunday roast. During particularly dull sermons her hand would surreptitiously find his and give his fingers a gentle squeeze.

The empty pew in which he now sat was a stark reminder

of his loneliness, just like the empty space beside him in bed which greeted him every morning. When he looked in the mirror, a careworn middle-aged man stared blankly back at him. As his dark hair gradually turned greyer and his face became more and more lined with age, he reflected that it was not just his wife that he had lost to his work, but also his youth.

He returned to the hotel feeling empty and slumped onto his bed. He leafed through the newspaper he had bought before the Claymore had left Glasgow but having already read it cover to cover, it offered nothing new.

Forrester hated inactivity. It was during such quiet moments that he found himself reflecting on the disappointments of his life. Always at the forefront of the growing list of disappointments was the day Lillian left. He cursed himself, remembering how he had been so obsessed with his work that he had not noticed the malaise of his home life. He closed his eyes and gently massaged the pulverised gristle that had once been his nose with the tips of his fingers.

His nose was his mark of shame. The day it had been broken marked the start of his obsession. The day he had finally caught the person responsible had not brought the tranquillity he had hoped for. Forrester had expected his anger to subside and that things would return to normal. By that time, however, Lillian had gone and all that he was left with was anger. Every time he looked in the mirror and saw his flattened nose was a reminder of his failure.

Tired of wallowing in self-pity, Forrester made his way downstairs to the hotel lounge. Now that the day's religious observances had been carried out, the lounge was warmed by a blazing fire and a number of the other guests of the hotel occupied the armchairs. Seating himself in a chair by the window, Forrester lit a cigarette and caught the attention of the lady who had chastised him that morning.

"What can I get ye?" she asked.

"A drink would be pleasant, if that isn't too much trouble."

"Would ye care for a dram?"

"That would be most agreeable," he answered. "Thank you."

She returned with the drink and leaned over to whisper in his ear.

"I hope I didnae give ye a fright this mornin'," she hissed conspiratorially. "It's chust that I cannae have smoke from the chimney before church. The neighbours would talk."

Once left alone, Forrester sipped his whisky and gazed out of the window at the young forest on the other side of the bay. A seagull flapped its wings and soared into the grey sky, circling the dark green of the trees before vanishing in the direction of the open sea. A steady rain began to fall, heavy droplets that drummed against the windowpane and rippled the calm water of the bay. The whisky tasted good. Having nothing better to do with his time, he ordered another.

Chapter 3

A grey streak of sunlight filtered through the gap in the curtain. Forrester lay tangled amidst the thick quilt and grimaced at the unwelcome shaft of light. His head ached and his mouth felt as though he had been chewing nettles. He reached to the glass that stood on the bedside table and swigged from it without checking its contents. Retching as he tasted the whisky, he kicked off the eiderdown and stumbled to the jug of water that stood on the dresser.

He gazed at his reflection in the mirror. Dark bags hung beneath his eyes, contradicting the early hour that he had retired to bed. He poured some of the cold water into the basin and splashed his face with it. Feeling no better, he stumbled back over to the bed and crawled beneath the covers.

Forrester was just beginning to drift off when a loud knock on the door jarred him back into consciousness.

"Who is it?" he groaned.

"Colin," the familiar voice answered. "Are ye gonna let me in or will ye keep me waitin' downstairs?"

"What time is it?" Forrester mumbled as he opened the door to let the young man into the room.

"It's three in the afternoon, ye've overslept! The boats will be sailin' soon," Colin snapped. "Look at yerself, man... Ye're in some state! And I thought ye wanted an early start!"

"I do," Forrester quickly fastened his tie and pulled on his greatcoat, "I'm ready."

"Ye look terrible," Colin chuckled. "Did ye over-indulge in the local waters by any chance?"

Ignoring Colin's laughter, Forrester led the way out of the room and marched them in the direction of North Beach. The weather was little better than the previous day. A dark grey cloud hung in the sky and a cruel wind blew against them all the way along Cromwell Street. Compared to the stillness of Sunday morning, the quayside at North Beach was a hive of activity. Men jostled past, staggering beneath the weight of the large nets which were loaded into the boats. The smaller boats that had rested on the beach were being lifted by their crews and carried into the water. Loud voices called out in Gaelic as sails were hoisted and the boats were made ready for departure. Forrester edged his way through the crowds, heading to where the Manannán had been anchored the day before.

"What's your plan?" Colin asked, raising his voice to be heard over the hum of the crowd.

"I want to talk to Macleod," Forrester answered, "get his side of the story."

Forrester did not need Colin's assistance to spot Murdo Macleod. He was a big man, tall and broad, with a dark shaggy beard streaked with grey hanging below his chin. He wore a pair of leather waders which reached up to his thighs and a heavy waterproof jacket that had turned a sickly yellow with age. He sat on a tall pile of barrels and barked orders to the men who carried the smaller boats from the shore to the water. It was clear from the large man's demeanour that he was in charge.

"Murdo Macleod?" Forrester called, looking up at the domineering figure.

Macleod ignored Forrester, continuing to holler instructions to the men paddling the boats in the water.

"Macleod?" Forrester repeated. "I need to talk with you."

"What d'ye want?" Macleod roared. "Can ye no' see I'm busy?"

"I want to ask you some questions about Alistair Mackinnon."

"Young Ali?" Macleod grunted and clambered down from the barrels.

Standing between Forrester and Colin, Macleod towered over them. Turning his back to Colin, he glared at Forrester.

"Are ye wi' the polis?" he sneered. "I already told them, the boy fell out an' got drowned."

"Can you tell me any more than that?" Forrester continued, undeterred by the man's tone. "I've come from Glasgow to investigate the matter."

"Sounds tae me that ye've come a way further than that, Englishman," Macleod retorted. "I cannae talk wi'ye the now, there's work tae be done."

The large man shouldered past Forrester and sauntered over the water's edge where the crew of the Manannán had piled dozens of the large cotton nets. Not wishing to be dismissed in such a manner, Forrester hurried after him.

"I must talk to you about the boy!"

"The boy's dead." Macleod lifted one of the heavy nets onto his shoulder and strode into the waters towards his boat.

Forrester shrugged off his greatcoat and splashed through the waves after him. The water was cold but he did not flinch, even when it reached the top of his thighs. He took one end of the folded net and helped Macleod manhandle it into the boat. More nets followed and Forrester lost count of how many were taken onboard the large boat. When they had finished, Macleod pulled himself onto the deck of the boat and looked down at Forrester.

"Are ye lookin' fer work?"

"No, Mister Macleod. I just wish to speak with you."

"There's nothin' tae talk about."

"A boy is dead. You were in charge of the boat he worked on. I would say that there most certainly is something to talk about."

Macleod said nothing but met Forrester's gaze. His eyes were small and dark and gave nothing away. A lesser man would have wilted beneath such a stare but Forrester was not so easily intimidated. He stuffed his hands into his pockets and stuck out his chin defiantly.

"I must talk with you."

"We'll be back in the morning," Macleod muttered. "I might talk to ye then."

"I'll be waiting," Forrester answered and waded back to the beach.

Colin stood waiting for him on the esplanade. He shook his head dazedly as Forrester approached.

"Look at yerself!" he exclaimed, pointing to Forrester's sodden trousers. "What d'ye think ye're doin'?"

"He didn't seem too keen to talk," Forrester answered, "I had to show him that I wasn't about to give up easily."

"Ye're cracked," Colin chuckled and handed him his coat.

They sat and watched the remaining fishermen carry their boats down to the water and paddle out of the shallows. Forrester saw Macleod pace back and forth on the deck of the Manannán, shouting orders to the men who followed them without hesitation. They hauled on the lines and sails were raised on the two masts.

The sails were unfurled and billowed as they caught the wind. Forrester could not help but be impressed as he watched the large boat swing around and head out to sea. The white sails grew smaller and smaller in the distance before vanishing behind the spit of land that stretched out across the mouth of the bay. A squat lighthouse sat on the cliffs there, guarding the entrance to the calmer waters.

"Arnish Point," Colin commented. "Ye can get a fair view o' the Minch from out there."

When the last of the boats had sailed out past the headland and vanished from sight Colin slapped Forrester on the shoulder and grinned.

"I'm guessin' ye've had more productive days."

"We're not finished yet. At least we got to meet Macleod. That's a start."

"Aye, an' he's no' likely tae forget ye in a hurry. Look at yerself! Are ye feet no' freezin'?"

"They'll dry," Forrester muttered as he leaned against a wall and poured the seawater from his boots. "And we'll be here when the boats come back in to see what Macleod has to say. In the meantime, we ought to take a wander round town and see if we can dig up a little information about him. You have a chat to the cooper, Nicolson's his name. Buy him a drink or two, see if you can't get him talking."

"What are ye gonna dae?"

Forrester tugged off his wet socks and wrung them out one by one. He pointed to a pair of crooked wooden buildings which stood by the quayside and looked in danger of an imminent collapse. They appeared to only remain upright by virtue of the fact that they were supported on one side by the brick wall of a sturdier construction. Plumes of smoke billowed from the gaps in their roofs and filled the harbour with the smell of kippers.

"I'll take a wander over to those smokehouses. There's bound to be a few working there whose paths have crossed Macleod's at one time or another. We'll take our supper at the hotel tonight. How does seven o'clock suit you? You can tell me everything you've learned over a good meal and a glass of wine."

***

Colin drained the last of the wine in his glass and reached across the table for the bottle.

"Thirsty work, this police business," he commented as he refilled his glass to the brim.

"Did you talk with Nicolson?"

"Aye, I did. He was down on North Beach watchin' over the gyurls at the farlins. The man's a blasted slave driver the way he works the poor lassies. Shoutin' an' bawlin' at 'em all the time. He didnae seem keen tae talk at first but when I suggested we take a wee dram he went along nae bother."

"Did he tell you anything about Macleod?"

"A wee bit." Colin shovelled a forkful of food into his mouth and spoke as he chewed. "Nicolson's been fillin' barrels wi' herring for near twenty years. Macleod brings him the fish. He's got other fishermen on his books an' all but he says Murdo Macleod is his best supplier. He's got five boats goin' out every night an' not one of 'em comes back empty in the mornin'."

"Is that uncommon?"

"Uncommon? It's unheard of, man! It's enough tae ken where the good fishing waters are an' tae get your nets in the water. Whether or no' a shoal o' herrin' swim intae them is another matter. Sometimes it chust comes down tae luck an' I've heard o' fishermen no' gettin' a good catch for weeks at a time."

"Does Nicolson have any idea how he does it?"

"He told me he disnae care even if the devil himself is scarin' the fishies intae the nets so long as he can fill his barrels."

"Tomorrow morning I want you to ask the other fishermen about him. Find out what he does that makes him so damn lucky."

Colin tore off a hunk of bread and set about mopping up the gravy on his plate before reaching over and doing the same to Forrester's.

"Hungry, are we?" Forrester smirked.

"Did ye learn anythin' at the smokehouses?"

"Not a huge amount, I'm afraid. Not a soul could speak English in the first one I went to. The second one was run by an old soak who seemed more interested in pouring whisky down his throat than talking. I offered to buy him a drink if he could tell me about Macleod but he just laughed and said that Macleod provides more than enough drink for the town. What do you make of that?"

Colin shifted in his seat and tugged at his long hair as he thought.

"I've heard o' fishermen from Loch Fyne takin' a jaunt over tae Skye an' fillin' their boats wi' whisky. The excise men ken full well what they're up tae but they cannae seem tae catch 'em. Some say that all the villages along the west coast are drinkin' untaxed whisky from the illegal stills on the islands."

"You think Macleod is involved in smuggling?"

"There's a lot o' water between here an' the mainland. Who can tell what he's up tae? I'll wager ye'd have a devil of a time tryin' tae pin anythin' on him."

That evening Forrester lay in bed and ran through the possible scenarios in his head. Young Ali Mackinnon was not aware of the whisky smuggling and started to ask too many questions. Perhaps he was aware of the smuggling but mentioned it to the wrong people. Either way, Macleod had acted decisively and taken the opportunity to rid himself of the boy. He sighed. Colin was right. If Macleod was involved in smuggling it would be near impossible to prove anything unless the excise men were to catch him red-handed. There would be a number of people in the community who would not want to see the flow of illegal whisky onto the island disrupted and would provide any number of alibis for him should the case ever come to trial.

Forrester switched off the lamp and pulled the bed covers

tightly around him. His years in the police force had taught him that very few cases were as straightforward as they first appeared, and this one was no exception.

***

Morning came and Forrester met Colin at North Beach before the first of the boats returned to unload their catch. They stood at the quayside in silence and smoked cigarette after cigarette as they watched a group of small white sails skirt the headland.

As the boats drew closer, Forrester could see that they were heavily laden with fish, sitting far lower in the water than when they had departed. As the boats were brought into the shallows the quayside burst into life. The fishermen leapt out and splashed through the water as they dragged the boats onto the beach. Crowds of people gathered round the boats and carried the catch ashore in wicker baskets. From the baskets, the herring were transferred to the vast wooden troughs that stood on the quayside.

Once filled with fish, the trough was surrounded by herring girls. Working in groups of three, they sorted, gutted and packed the fish into barrels. The journey of the fish from the trough to the barrel was a swift, brutal one. The youngest of the girls sorted the fish, choosing the best of the herring for the top and bottom of the barrels. They handed the fish to the girl whose fingers were bound with strips of cloth. A knife would flash, the innards would be removed and the fish would be handed to the girl who carefully packed it in the barrel of salt. The whole process took mere seconds and an entire barrel could be filled in little over a minute. The girls laughed and chattered as they worked, never slowing their pace.

Forrester's eyes searched their faces, looking for the young woman he had spoken to on Sunday morning. Eventually, he spotted her at the far side of the group. She was engaged in gutting the fish, wielding the knife with quick, confident cuts. She wore a bloodstained apron to protect her clothes and her dark hair was still held back with a scarf. The young girl sorting the fish beside her said something. Effie responded with a smile before throwing her head back and beginning to sing.

Cò nì mire rium, hù hoireann ò,
Cò nì mire rium, ò hì abh ò,
Cò nì mire rium?

Hearing the familiar tune, the other girls at work joined in the singing, their voices carrying over the hum of the crowd on the quayside. Though Forrester could not understand the words, he was transported by the sweet voices and the steady rhythm of the song that seemed to match the pace at which the girls worked.

Cò nì sùgradh, cò nì cinnealtas?
Hù hoireann ò:

Cò nì mire rium, hù hoireann ò,
Cò nì mire rium, ò hi abh ò,
Cò nì mire rium?

Cò nì e mur dèan na gillean e?
Hù hoireann ò:

Cò nì mire rium, hù hoireann ò,
Cò nì mire rium, ò hi abh ò,
Cò nì mire rium?

"What are they singing about?" he asked Colin.

"Cò nì mire rium?" Colin smiled. "They're wonderin' who will sport wi' em. Same as all the songs the lassies sing, it's about boys."

The morning passed slowly. Forrester and Colin sat on a pile of barrels which gave them a good view of the harbour and watched the herring girls work, the supply of fish in the troughs replenished by the boats returning from the fishing grounds. At eleven o'clock Colin went to a nearby shop and bought a couple of steaming hot mutton pies that they ate out in the open, still waiting for the return of Macleod's boat.

By midday Colin was bored and wandered away from North Beach in search of other entertainments. Forrester remained where he was, his eyes fixed on the horizon for the tall sails of the Manannán. Stopping for a break, the herring girls moved away from the barrels and picked at their meagre lunches. Having spotted Forrester, Effie wandered over to him.

"Here again?" she asked, wiping her brow with the back of her hand and leaving a streak of blood across her forehead. "Ye must like it here."

"It's not so quiet as Sunday," he smiled. "I came yesterday to speak to Macleod. He said he'd give me some time when he returned."

"He did?" Effie raised her eyebrows in surprise. "Good luck to ye. He's a man o' few words an' fewer manners. Why d'ye want tae talk wi' Macleod?"

"A family matter," Forrester answered.

"Have ye family here?"

"In a manner of speaking, yes."

She chuckled as she tightened the bindings around her fingers.

"Ye're no' so talkative yourself, are ye? You an' Macleod'll get on chust fine!"

"Why do you girls tie your fingers in cloth?" he asked.

"My cloots?" she wiggled her digits and giggled. "They're tae stop me cuttin' myself wi' the knife. It stings like the devil when ye get salt in there. Some gyurls cut theyself bad an' the salt stops the wound from healin'. A friend o' mine, Mary, her hands got so bad she couldnae work anymore an' had tae go back an' live wi' her parents on their croft."

"Do you live in the town?"

"Aye," she pointed towards the narrow lanes that separated the two beaches of the quayside. "I share a room wi' four o' the gyurls over on Castle Lane. It's no' much but we're close tae the work. I used tae walk in from Beinn na Saighde but I couldnae get here early enough."

Their conversation was interrupted by the cry of "Tie fingers!" from a stout gentleman standing by the trough. Effie looked over her shoulder and sighed.

"That's Boabie Nicolson," she groaned. "Time for me to get back tae work. Bye then."

Forrester watched the young woman saunter back to the trough where she exchanged a few excited words with her peers before they resumed work. Digging in his pocket for his cigarette case, he turned his attention back to the mouth of the bay.

It was another half hour before Forrester spotted the vast sails of the Manannán appear from behind Arnish Point. He paced the beach impatiently whilst he waited for Macleod's arrival. His irritation grew when he realised that Macleod had no intention of speaking to him straight away. The large man waded to the shore and exchanged words with Boabie Nicolson before supervising the unloading of his catch. Only when the herring girls were engaged in gutting and packing the fish did Macleod stroll across the beach to where Forrester waited.

"Good catch?" Forrester asked.

"An ceann no bliadhna a dh'innseas an t-iagsgair iasgach," Macleod answered. Seeing the confusion on Forrester's face he translated for him. "It is at the end of the year that the fisherman tells of his fishin'."

Forrester extended his hand and Macleod grasped it firmly. His skin was rough and calloused and his grip was that of a man who wishes the other to know that he is in charge. He eyed Forrester with suspicion before he spoke.

"Well?" he snapped. "Ye've got me here, what d'ye want to ask me?"

"Tell me about Alistair Mackinnon."

"The boy?" Macleod sniffed. "He came tae work on my boat in August. He was keen tae learn and quiet. That's two qualities I admire in a lad so I kept him on."

"What happened to him?"

"The boy fell out an' got drowned, I told ye," Macleod scowled.

"Can you be more specific?"

"September is the end o' the season, d'ye ken? We have tae go further tae catch the herring," the big man explained. "We'd gone out past Pairc, almost down tae Harris. Storm came up so we decided tae take the boat intae Loch Sealg an' wait for it tae pass. The wind was against us so we were beating against it. A large wave hit the boat an' wee Ali fell out. The tide must've caught him 'cause by the time we'd turned about tae pick him up he was gone."

"Most unfortunate." Forrester lit a cigarette and offered the case to Macleod. "Would you be able to take me to where the boy fell out?"

Macleod took a cigarette and placed it between his lips.

"That would depend on how useful ye could make yerself on the boat," he grinned. "D'ye ken?"

"I'll admit that I don't know the first thing about sailing," Forrester reached into his pocket and withdrew a handful of coins. "But whatever money you lose in trade I will reimburse."

He jingled the coins in his hand whilst Macleod eyed them greedily. The large man's ruddy cheeks flushed a darker shade of red as he relented.

"Very well," he muttered. "Be here before we sail tomorrow evenin' an dinnae wear yer finest. I'll take ye out there but I cannae say it'll be cheap."

Forrester stood on the quayside for the rest of the afternoon and watched the fishermen at work. Once the catch was unloaded, the wet nets were hauled off the boat and hung out to dry. Macleod and his crew spent a couple of hours in the quayside pubs before returning to the beach laden with another set of nets which were loaded onto the boats as before. Unlike the other fishermen, Macleod's crew did not seem in a hurry to get out of the harbour and back to the fishing grounds. They stood about on the beach, talking amongst themselves and whistling at the herring girls. The setting sun was turning the sky a deep purple by the time Macleod called his crew aboard and they hoisted the Manannán's sails into place. Lanterns were lit fore and aft on the boat and she nosed her way out of the harbour at a leisurely pace. Forrester watched the lights of the boat grow smaller and smaller until they vanished into the darkness.

Chapter 4

"I cannae allow it," Maggie Mackinnon slammed the plate down in front of Forrester. "Murdo Macleod is no' a man tae be trusted."

"Maggie," Calum said, placing a hand on his wife's arm in an attempt to quieten her, "the good inspector is chust tryin' tae help us."

"I don't want another body floatin' in the Minch on my behalf," she pouted. "Macleod is a killer. I wouldnae walk in front o' him, let alone get intae his boat."

Forrester was taking an early supper with Colin at the home of Calum Mackinnon and his wife. Their small cottage was in the village of Lacasdail, a half hour's walk from the town. Upon arrival, Maggie Mackinnon had made every effort to accommodate their guests, heaping more coals on the fire and refilling their glasses of Scotch without being asked. Sitting in the warmth of the small room they had been entertained by the clumsy dances performed by Heather, the Mackinnons' young daughter.

As in so many Scottish homes, time was measured in

glasses of whisky. Calum returned from his croft a short time after they had finished their third glass and joined the men beside the fire. He kicked off his muddy boots with a sigh and collapsed into the comfortable chair, his black and white border collie curled up by his feet.

As the food was being served, Forrester had told the family of his conversation with Murdo Macleod the previous afternoon. Maggie, still grieving from the loss of her son, had not taken the news well.

"What would you have me do?" Forrester asked. "I want to get closer to the man. I must find out more about him before I can take the investigation any further."

"What d'ye need tae know?" Maggie sniffed as she dabbed her eyes with the corner of a napkin. "He killed my boy."

"Did he?" Forrester spoke quietly. "How can you be sure it was not an accident as Macleod says? From what I've heard no body has yet been found. How can you be so certain that it was foul play?"

Calum laid his knife and fork down on the table and fixed Forrester with a hostile stare.

"Macleod told ye about the storm?"

Forrester nodded.

"There wasnae any storm. Near two hundred boats were out on the Minch that day an no' one other saw any sign o' bad weather."

"You cannot accuse the man of murder just because of that!" Forrester snorted. "I agreed to help you look further into the matter but we can't leap to conclusions."

Maggie rose from the table and began gathering the empty plates. Her shaking hands did not pass unnoticed and Colin leapt to his feet to help. As they carried the crockery away Calum leant across the table and whispered to Forrester.

"We do appreciate ye comin' here, Inspector," he intoned. "And of course ye must carry out yer investigation how ye see fit. But ye must believe us. Macleod is no' a kind man. There are some who hold that he's in league wi' the devil. His boats always bring in the best catches. It's like he's blessed. Macleod has never lost a boat, never even lost a mast in ill weather."

"But he lost your son," Forrester interjected.

"Precisely," Calum banged the table with his fist. "But he wasnae lost. He was given as a gift tae the sea. He was a sacrifice."

***

Forrester arrived at North Beach just before six o'clock. Although the sun was still visible above the rooftops of the town, the clear skies hinted at a cold night ahead. Forrester shivered, regretting his decision to go out on Macleod's boat. Though he wore a heavy knit jumper and a scarf beneath his greatcoat, the breeze seemed to pass right through him. As always at this time of day, the quayside was busy with fishermen preparing their nets and hauling their boats into the waters.

He found Murdo Macleod sitting on the pile of barrels, supervising the launching of his boats and bellowing orders at all who would listen. Seeing Forrester approach, the large man climbed down and removed the pipe that hung from his mouth.

"Ye're late," he said, prodding Forrester with the stem of the pipe. "Two of my boats have already sailed."

Forrester offered empty apologies as he followed Macleod down to the water's edge. The nets had already been loaded onto the Manannán and she bobbed on the gentle waves a dozen yards from the shore. Two men waited in the bows of the boat and they stared as Forrester and Macleod approached the edge of the water.

Macleod waded into the water, calling out in Gaelic to the men who watched them. Forrester removed his boots, rolled up his trousers and followed. Once they reached the boat they clambered over the side with the assistance of those already onboard. Two more men waded out to the boat and were helped onto the deck. Macleod exchanged a few curt words in Gaelic to the four men before he turned to Forrester.

"These lads are my crew on the Manannán. Jeck Macphail, Wullie Ross, Seumas Maciver an' Rowan Campbell."

The men threw Forrester cold glances as he greeted them. They remained silent as they rowed the boat out into deeper waters. Forrester sat himself on a pile of netting to the stern and tried to remain as unobtrusive as possible whilst the men prepared the boat to sail. Macleod gave the signal and two of the men began to pull on the halyard, raising the heavy wooden yard attached to the massive sail sixty feet up. Once secured, the men tightened the lines and allowed the wind to fill the large white sails.

The boat began to move with the wind, steadily at first but quickly picking up speed. Soon, the Manannán was skimming across the water and heading for the mouth of the bay. Leaving Macphail to call out instructions to the other men, Macleod moved over to Forrester and lit his pipe.

"A good day," he muttered, the glow from the pipe's bowl lighting his dark features. "The wind is wi' us. We should be able tae get out tae the fish before the others."

"The fish?" Forrester asked. "I thought you were showing me where the boy was lost."

"All in good time." Macleod puffed away on the pipe. "This is a workin' boat an' we're no' used tae carryin' passengers. First we'll catch some fish an' then we'll head out tae Sruth nam Fear Gorm."

As Macleod spoke, it did not escape Forrester's notice that the two sailors within earshot exchanged worried glances.

"To where?" Forrester asked.

"The Sound o' Shiant... Sruth nam Fear Gorm is what we Islanders call it."

"What does it mean?"

"Stream o' Wee Fishies." Macleod cleared his throat and spat into the foaming waters before turning his attention to the horizon.

The boat glided past the squat lighthouse atop Arnish Point, out of the mouth of the bay and into the choppier water of the Minch. The wind was stronger now and the boat bounced over the wave-strewn sea. Determined not to get seasick as he had on the crossing from Glasgow, Forrester took deep breaths and kept his eyes fixed on the jagged rocks of the shoreline. It did not take Macleod long to notice his discomfort.

"D'ye no' like boats?" he chuckled.

"Not so much the boats," Forrester muttered, "it's the sea I'm not so keen on."

"The sea can be cruel, that much is true," Macleod said thoughtfully as he looked out at the expanse of blue glittering in the pale evening light. "But she provides many wi' a livin'. She can be generous one day and mean the next. Ye can gae out on a calm sea an' come back wi' a squall at yer back. I've seen many a boat taken by the Minch when she's in a foul mood. I've seen waves as tall as Beinn Mhòr lift a Fifie boat an' drop it chust as fast. Nae fear, mind. Ye're in safe hands wi' the Manannán."

"She's a fine boat," Forrester answered, swallowing the bile that rose in his throat.

"Fine?" Macleod snorted, "She's the finest, man. There's nae faster from here tae Skye. She's a Zulu, no' two years old."

"A Zulu?"

"Aye," Macleod continued proudly, "she may be long but she's got a short keel an' can turn quicker than most smaller boats. She's fast too. Ten knots wi' a good wind behind her."

"I see she has a deck too," Forrester commented. "That must be handy in a storm."

"Ye've good eyes," Macleod replied. "A deck is both a blessin' an' a curse. Ye can take shelter in foul weather, that's true. But ye cannae always shelter when there's work tae be done. In a Skaffie boat ye may have nae shelter but ye can brace yersel' against a thwart. Wi' a deck ye cannae do that. Chust wan slip an' ye're in the water, d'ye ken?"

"Is that what happened to the boy?"

Macleod nodded and barked an order in Gaelic to the sailors. Macphail, the shortest and stockiest member of the crew, let one of the lines out and as the sail swung round to the starboard side the boat turned so that the coastline was behind them.

"There's good fishin' further out," Macleod explained as they watched the cliffs shrink into the distance.

They sailed for another hour before they dropped the sails and allowed the boat to drift on the current. By that time the sun had set and it was bitterly cold on the open waters. Macleod tapped out the contents of his pipe and clapped his hands.

"A perfect tide," he remarked. "Chust perfect. These are fine waters for herrin' an' there's no' another boat for miles."

Forrester helped the men push the large nets overboard and watched as they drifted alongside the boat. Having cast the nets in the water, the men made themselves comfortable on the deck, smoking and chatting in Gaelic to pass the time. Knowing no Gaelic himself, Forrester was left out of the conversation, only able to contribute when Macleod offered his services as a translator. The other men on the boat did not seem to understand English, and if they did, they made no effort to speak it. Forrester smoked his cigarettes incessantly, impatient for the time when they would collect the nets back in and make their way over to the area Macleod had called Sruth nam Fear Gorm.

After a time, the fishermen began to play a game of chance using a pair of well worn whalebone dice. The rules seemed needlessly complicated and Forrester watched money change hands as frequently as the dice were rolled. Macleod did not join in the game but swaggered over to where Forrester sat.

"D'ye no' fancy tryin' a game?"

Forrester shook his head.

"I don't play."

"Would ye care for a dram?"

Without waiting for a response Macleod opened the hatch that led beneath the deck. It was too dark for Forrester to see what went on below but he heard the sound of many bottles clinking. A short time later Macleod emerged holding a large bottle of whisky.

"No cups on this boat," he smiled and took a swig from the bottle. "Ye'll chust have tae drink like the rest o' us."

Forrester was handed the bottle and took a mouthful. It was coarse but not altogether unpleasant and it momentarily banished the cold he felt nipping at him. He looked at the plain bottle in the dim light of the lantern.

"There's no label. Whose malt is this?"

Macleod shrugged and took the bottle from him. He replaced the cork and tossed it across the boat to the other men.

"That wouldn't be illegally distilled whisky, would it?"

The large man sat himself by Forrester's side and nudged him with his elbow.

"There's no harm done wi' a wee bit o' peatreek between friends, is there?"

"I heard more than a few bottles below decks."

"I've more'n a few friends."

Forrester gazed out into the darkness. There were no other boats nearby, at least no other boats that were signalling their presence with lanterns. He had grown used to the gentle rise and fall of the boat on the waves, what unnerved him was the distance from land should anything happen. The darkness had robbed him of all sense of direction and he had no idea in which direction the island lay.

"Tell me about the fishing season."

"What ye see at the moment is nothin'. It disnae start in earnest till next month but then ye can barely see the water in the harbour for boats."

"I'm told your catches are always good."

Macleod could not disguise the smile that momentarily softened his hard features.

"Aye, that they are. But they're better in season. A wise man can make a fortune fishin' these waters."

"Have you made a fortune?"

"I'm no' a poor man but there's always money still tae be made."

"Are there many other men with four fishing boats at their command?"

"Five," Macleod corrected him with pride. "An' a further twenty five comin' o'er from the East coast next month tae work under me for the season."

"That's a lot of boats."

Macleod roared with laughter and pushed himself to his feet.

"It's a start, but it's no' enough. I'm a man o' vision, y'ken? I won't be satisfied until all the fish pulled out o' the Minch is done so by my boats an' only my boats!"

It was several more hours before the nets were hauled in. Most of the crew drifted off to sleep but Macleod remained awake, pacing the deck and whistling through his teeth. Forrester tried to sleep but the motion of the boat and the cold night air kept him awake. By the time the fishermen began to rouse themselves he was feeling eager to partake in some form of activity and volunteered to help by manning the capstan, the hand winch which hauled in the lines. The winch was stiff and Forrester was required to lend his strength to the labour. His hands began to blister after a few dozen turns of the winch and his arms and shoulders were soon aching terribly. A few feet of the net would be pulled in at a time. The caught fish would be removed and sorted before the next couple of feet of netting came aboard. When the catch was finally heaped on a tarpaulin beneath the deck, the crew turned their attention to another net and the whole painful process was repeated. When the final net had been brought in, Forrester collapsed to the deck and plunged his blistered hands into a bucket of cold water. Macleod and his sailors ignored him as they raised the sails and the boat once more began to skip across the waves.

"Are we heading there now?" Forrester shouted, his voice muffled by the wind. "Where the boy was lost?"

"We are," Macleod answered as he refilled his pipe. "But we'll no' get there for a time yet."

"Is it far?"

"That it is. More'n two hours even wi' a good wind."

Forrester groaned and sat himself on the wet pile of netting. The sailors chattered to one another in Gaelic as they steered the boat across the expansive sea. Macleod leant against the mast and watched him, a wry smile creasing his weathered features.

"Something funny, Macleod?" he asked, his irritation evident.

"Ye're no' a patient man, are ye?" Macleod scoffed. "Is that how your neb came to be so crooked? I daresay the other chap came off nae better."

Ignoring the comment, Forrester looked at the coastline in the distance and lit another cigarette.

"Tell me about the tides that day," he spoke after a time. "I understand the boy didn't wash up on the shore."

"The tides?" Macleod grimaced. "Explainin' the tides tae ye wouldnae be possible. Ye dinnae ken these waters. There's no' one tide, but several. The Sound o' Shiant is one o' the worst stretches o' water I've ever sailed. Ye've one tide sweepin' down from the North East an' another comin' up from the South West an' they meet chust in that strait 'tween the Long Island an' the Shiants. I'm no' surprised the boy hasnae washed up, I'd be gey surprised if he did."

"The Shiants?" Forrester sat up. "What are they?"

"A handful o' small islands," Macleod waved a hand dismissively. "I've never had reason tae visit them. Chust one family an' their flock o' sheep. Good fishin' nearby by few dare tae risk those tides."

"Is there a chance the boy could have washed up on the islands?"

"Aye, there's a chance." Macleod exhaled and watched the smoke linger in the air between them. "But Domhnall Mor – that's what they call the shepherd – Big Donald, he'd hae foun' the body."

"Is there any way to visit the islands?"

"I'm no' goin' over there," Macleod said, shaking his head, "The Manannán's no' a pleasure yacht, y'ken?"

Though Forrester pressed Macleod for further information about the islands and the tides around the Sound of Shiant, the fisherman was less than forthcoming with his responses. They filled their empty bellies with salted herring and hardtack, washing the sparse breakfast down with milk drunk from a battered can that was passed around the men. The sky was beginning to lighten and Forrester breathed a sigh of relief when Campbell pointed out a series of dark shapes which rose out of the water on the horizon.

"Na h-Eileanan Seunta," Campbell mumbled.

Forrester did not need Macleod to translate. He knew that the tall black cliffs he could see silhouetted against the early morning sky were the Shiant Isles. He looked around them at the gently rolling waves and the gulls which flapped lazily after the boat in search of food.

"This is the Sound of Shiant?" he smiled.

"It may look calm the now," Macleod scowled, "but if ye were tae see this in a storm, ye'd shit your trousers. I'm no' jestin' when I say these waters is cruel."

"I don't doubt it." Forrester bit his lip. "Can you show me where the boy fell out?"

Macleod looked past Forrester at the stretch of water lying between the islands and the mainland. His lip curled as he chewed the stem of his pipe. Turning, he called a few Gaelic words to Macphail who gave a similarly curt answer.

"We're goin' nae further," he sniffed, "I dinnae like the look o' it."

"But it's as calm as anything!" Forrester laughed.

"D'ye no' listen, man?" Macleod's face twisted with rage as he shouted. "I'm goin' nae further! Ye may be polis on the mainland but this is my boat an' ye'll dae what I says unless ye'd rather swim back."

Silenced by Macleod's outburst, Forrester stared at the dark waters. Macleod shouted some orders in Gaelic and the sailors took hold of a drift net and cast it into the sea.

"You're fishing again?" Forrester asked incredulously.

"Aye," Macleod spat, "this is a fishin' boat, in case ye didnae notice."

The sun had risen by the time the net was hauled back in

and the catch was added to the already substantial pile beneath the deck. Forrester's patience had run out around the same time as his supply of cigarettes. Though Campbell and Macphail had raised the sails, the canvas hung limply from the masts.

"What now?" he scowled.

"Wind's dropped," Macleod answered, his eyes on the horizon. "If there's no wind we're no' goin' anywhere."

The boat rocked gently as Forrester scrambled to his feet and stood beside Macleod.

"What do you mean?" he hissed. "So we're just going to sit here twiddling our thumbs until the tide takes us onto those rocks?"

"Have ye a pocket knife?"

"What has that got to do with it?"

"Have ye got one or no'?"

Forrester shook his head.

Macleod muttered something under his breath as he searched his own pockets. Finding nothing, he swore and called to Macphail. The younger man hurried over to Macleod's side and exchanged a few words in Gaelic. Though not tall, Macphail was well built and moved with familiarity on the deck of the boat. Forrester guessed that he was in his early twenties but Macphail's thick stubble and woollen hat hindered any further scrutiny.

Macphail pulled a knife from his belt and handed it to Macleod. Turning away without a word of thanks, Macleod weighed the blade in his hands. He moved to the largest mast and stuck the knife into the solid wood. Satisfied with his work, he took a seat on the deck and began filling his pipe.

"What did you do that for?" Forrester asked.

Macleod smirked and pointed with the stem of his pipe to the lines which hung slack before them. Forrester watched with amazement as a gentle breeze began to stir them. Macleod lit his pipe and watched the smoke catch a gust of wind and drift away.

"There's always a wind," he smiled as the sails began to fill. "Ye chust have tae ask for it right."

***

Colin McCormick stared at Forrester as he poured himself a cup of coffee from the steaming pot. Although it was late in the morning the hotel lounge was full of shadows, the spluttering gas lamps providing scant light. Colin did not have to see his companion's face to know that he was talking in earnest.

"I'm no Hielan'," he muttered, "but that's no' natural. Sounds like witchery tae me."

"Whatever it was," Forrester stared at his untouched breakfast as he spoke, "it got us back to Stornoway damned quickly. I was glad to be off that boat after all that time in Macleod's company."

"Did ye find what ye wanted?"

"Not really," Forrester sniffed. "He took me close by where Alistair was lost, but he refused to go any further into the Sound of Shiant."

"That's no' good waters from what I hear," Colin commented.

"Well they were as calm as anything today and he still

refused. If the man wasn't such an insufferable brute I'd say that he was afraid of it. The others onboard didn't seem too pleased about going there. I think you're right about the smuggled whisky. It sounded like he was carrying several crates of bottles below decks but I didn't get a good look."

"D'ye think Macleod killed wee Ali?"

Forrester leaned back in his seat and sighed. He ran one hand across his eyes and down the pulverised bridge of his nose.

"I don't know," he stated. "He gave me a number of good reasons to believe that it was an accident. Fishing is not the safest of professions and the boy was relatively inexperienced..."

"Ye dinnae believe him, d'ye?"

"There was something about those islands that he wanted to stay away from. Before I talk to him again I think I ought to go over there. Do you think we could charter a boat?"

"Aye," Colin shrugged, "if ye've got the money I dinnae see why no'. I can ask some o' the fishermen at the harbour before they set out this evenin'."

Forrester reached into his pocket and scattered a number of coins onto the table before them.

"You go and see if you can get one for tomorrow," he said, sorting through the coins before pushing five shillings across the table to Colin. "A cheap one, mind, Macleod's cost me a small fortune."

Colin reached over and helped himself to a fried sausage from Forrester's plate then snatched up the coins.

"I'll see what I can dae," he smiled.

"I think it best that we don't tell Calum and his wife about what happened today."

Colin nodded as he pulled on his coat and bade Forrester farewell. Once alone, Forrester poured himself another coffee and considered the events of the night. The incident with the knife and the mast had certainly been strange but in his forty-four years he had encountered many strange things that most rational men would scoff at.

Science had not yet unravelled all the mysteries of nature and Forrester had experienced situations that defied both logic and explanation. Any attempt at rationalising such events had met with little success and eventually, he had stopped searching for answers to the unexplainable. He did know that if Calum or Maggie Mackinnon were to hear of Macleod's ability to summon a wind it would only further vindicate their belief that the man was in league with dark forces.

His thoughts were interrupted by the arrival of Calum himself. The heavy-set man was accompanied by his dog who curled up at her master's feet and fell asleep almost immediately. Calum took a sniff of Colin's half empty cup of coffee and wrinkled his nose in disgust.

"Well?" he asked. "Ye made it back then?"

"I'm here, aren't I?"

"D'ye think he did it?" Calum continued eagerly. "D'ye believe Macleod killed my boy?"

"I don't know what to believe at present," Forrester stated, "but there isn't any firm evidence that points a finger of blame at Macleod."

Calum cleared his throat and folded his arms across his broad chest.

"Well, what did ye learn?"

"Very little, I'm afraid." Forrester spoke carefully to avoid further upsetting his companion. "Macleod didn't really tell me anything I didn't know already and any questions I asked his crew had to be translated by him so I can't even be sure of the answers I did receive."

"So, it was a waste o' time."

"Not entirely," Forrester continued. "They took me out close by to the spot Alistair was lost. There are some islands there that I plan to visit."

"Islands?" Calum started. "What islands?"

"The Shiants. Alistair was lost in the straits near there, Sruth nam something something."

"Fear Gorm," Calum nodded solemnly, "Sruth nam Fear Gorm."

"That's it! Sruth nam Fear Gorm," Forrester repeated. "The Stream of Little Fish. Colin and I are going to head out there tonight and-"

"What did ye call it?" Calum interrupted. "The Stream o' Little Fish? That's no' what Sruth nam Fear Gorm means!"

"Isn't it?" Forrester shrugged. "Perhaps he said Wee Fish, I don't recall."

"It doesnae mean anythin' about fish!" Calum hissed. "Sruth nam Fear Gorm means The Stream o' Blue Men!"

Chapter 5

"What do you mean nobody?" Forrester asked incredulously.

"Chust that," Colin shrugged, "I asked about but couldnae find a soul that'd take us there."

"Did they give you any reason?"

"No' much. Some said that it wouldnae be worth their time. Most chust laughed at the idea, they said they'd sooner sail intae the mouth o' hell than gae near the Shiants. It seems Macleod has all rights on fishin' that straight. The other men dinnae want tae tread on his toes, y'ken?"

"How can he have rights on the sea?" Forrester lit a cigarette and offered one to Colin. "I didn't think it worked that way..."

"It disnae," Colin replied, "but Macleod's name seems tae swing a lot o' weight an' accordin' tae the other fishermen, he works those waters."

Forrester ran a hand over his chin as he thought. If the other fishermen refused to take him out to the Shiants, he would have to return to Macleod and ask him again. He looked at his pocket-watch and saw that it was close to nine o'clock in the evening. The activities of the previous night had left him exhausted but he had foregone sleep in favour of continuing his investigations into Macleod's business.

"Did ye learn anythin' this mornin'?"

"I tried to have a talk to the Chief Magistrate. It was hard enough getting to meet the man, I had to lie and say that I was on official police business. Fortunately his secretary was the most obsequious little toad I've ever met and made the arrangements."

"What did the Chief Magistrate tell ye?"

"Nothing we haven't heard a dozen times already. The same old story about the storm and how the boy slipped overboard. I don't trust the man for a moment. He's a merchant by trade and seems more interested in making money than administering the laws of the land. You should of seen his face when I asked to see the reports on young Ali's death. It was like I'd asked him to pull the stars from the sky. He spent about twenty minutes conferring in Gaelic with that damned secretary before he muttered something about the files going missing and that I would have to excuse him because he was a very busy man."

"Another waste o' time then," Colin groaned.

"Not entirely. Remember I told you about the bottles of whisky without labels on Macleod's boat? The Chief Magistrate poured me a drink from a similar bottle. Now I'm no expert on whisky, but I'd swear that it was the same malt."

"If the Chief Magistrate's in Macleod's pocket then there's no' a chance o' provin' a thing against the man!"

"That may be so on the island but Macleod wouldn't be able to bribe a court on the mainland. I'm not finished yet. Now, I must get some sleep and we'll pay Mister Macleod another visit in the morning."

He stood up to leave when Colin spoke again.

"Och, I almos' forgot," he exclaimed, "there was a lassie at North Beach askin' after ye."

"A woman?"

"Aye," Colin winked, "a gey fine one too. She asked if I was wi' the Englishman. I told her that it was fairer tae say that the Englishman was wi' me."

"Morrison?" Forrester asked. "Was that her name?"

"Aye, that it was. D'ye ken the lassie? She wanted tae talk wi' ye at North Beach. She wouldnae tell me any more."

"Will she be there now?"

"Ye can try. If ye cannae find her on North Beach ye could try one o' the pubs," Colin chuckled. "I dinnae suppose ye'll be needin' me?"

"No, thank you," Forrester replied. "You head back to Calum's house and meet me here in the morning. I'll go and talk to her myself."

***

Stifling his yawns, Forrester hurried along Cromwell Street. Flickering gas lamps bathed the road in a warm light but North Beach was shrouded in darkness. Forrester wandered between the stacks of barrels and allowed his eyes to adjust to the lack of light. He could hear the waves breaking nearby and smell the pungent aromas of seaweed and smoked fish. Rubbing his hands together to keep them warm, he watched his breath hang in the cold air before him.

The shingle of North Beach seemed naked when the fishermen's boats were out plying their trade. Other than a few rats that scavenged amongst the seaweed the beach was deserted. Forrester walked over to the trough where he had seen Effie and the other herring girls at work. The noise of his boots walking over the pebbles disturbed the stillness of the night and seemed to echo all around him. The trough was empty and rather than returning the way he had come, Forrester perched himself on the rim and smoked a cigarette.

He listened to the sound of the waves and could discern the faint sound of singing coming from a nearby pub. Remembering Colin's advice on where he might find Effie he flicked the end of the cigarette away and rose to his feet. In no particular hurry, he thrust his hands into his pockets and trudged along the beach. As he reached the piles of barrels he heard something to his right and paused. A rumbling sound caused him to glance upwards before his reflexes took over.

Forrester dived to one side as a barrel smashed into the ground where he had been standing and broke open, spilling its contents of salted herring onto the ground. Another barrel fell from the pile and missed Forrester by inches.

Bellowing with rage, Forrester pushed himself to his feet and scrambled over the pile of barrels in search of whoever had tried to crush him. One barrel falling could have been dismissed as an accident, but the second had confirmed that someone had deliberately pushed them. As he clambered onto the highest point of the stack he saw a figure scurrying away into the shadows beneath him.

Without pausing to think of his own safety, Forrester leapt from the pile. Despite rolling as he hit the ground, the wind was still knocked out of him and he wheezed as he followed the figure into the gloomy passage between two towering walls of barrels.

A fist connected with Forrester's jaw and knocked him off his feet. The figure stepped out of a hidden alcove and loomed over him. Seeing a knife glitter in the moonlight, Forrester responded quickly and kicked out at the figure's legs. His foot caught his assailant behind the knee and caused the leg to buckle. By the time the figure had recovered his balance Forrester was back on his feet. The knife sliced through the air and Forrester skipped backwards to avoid the blade, remaining out of reach until he saw his opportunity. In one swift movement he lunged forward and grabbed hold of his attacker's arm. Up close, he clung to the man and slammed the hand against the barrels until the knife was dropped. Now disarmed, the man grappled Forrester and drove him into the wall.

Gasping for breath, Forrester saw the man reach for the blade lying just out of reach. He kicked out and struck his opponent's arm then hurled himself at him. He struck the man over and over, his blows raining down until the figure lay still beneath him.

Forrester reached for the knife and held it to the dazed man's neck. Breathing heavily, he hauled the dead weight out of the shadows and stared at the battered face in the dim moonlight. Though the man's face was bruised and bleeding Forrester recognised him immediately.

"Why did you attack me?" Forrester snarled as he shook Jack Macphail. "Tell me!"

Macphail moaned through thick lips and spat a mouthful of blood. Forrester shook him once more and pressed the knife harder against his throat.

"Tell me, you useless Scotch bastard," he hissed, "or I'll cut your god-damned throat and leave your body for the gulls."

"Chan eil mi a' tuigsinn," Macphail mumbled as he hung limply in Forrester's grip.

Forrester released his hold on the man's collar and watched him slump to the ground. Not understanding a word of Gaelic, he knew that he would be unable to get any information from him. He planted a firm kick in the man's abdomen before turning his back on the groaning body and returning to the hotel on Cromwell Street.

He woke the next morning to find that he ached all over. His back was bruised and his jaw hurt from the blow that caught him off-guard. Ten years ago, he would have been able to take such a brawl in his stride. Now in the grip of middle age, Forrester found that vigorous activity left his muscles throbbing and his joints complaining. Flexing his swollen knuckles, he groggily recalled the incident and thought about what his next move should be.

Having washed and dressed, he made his way downstairs and ate a light breakfast. He had just eaten the last slice of toast when Colin strode into the lounge and joined him at the table.

"Holy smokes, man!" he laughed. "Did ye get in a tussle wi' the gyurl? An' there was me thinkin' ye was a gentleman!"

"She wasn't there," Forrester answered coldly, not sharing Colin's mirth. "One of Macleod's boys attacked me on North Beach."

"I'm sorry... I shouldnae have left ye."

"Don't be daft," Forrester drained the last of his coffee. "I took care of it. Macphail won't be troubling anyone else for a while."

"And Macleod?" Colin asked. "What o' him?"

"We leave him for now. I'm more interested in what Effie Morrison has to say for herself."

There were no signs of the previous night's affray at North Beach. The broken barrels had been tidied away and the shoreline was once again crowded with boats and workers. By the time Colin and Forrester arrived a number fishermen had already landed their catch and the herring girls were hard at work gutting and packing the fish. Having told Colin to stay put, Forrester shouldered his way through the crowd and grabbed Effie by the arm.

"I want to talk to you," he hissed as he pulled her aside.

"Hoi!" an angry voice called out. "Ye cannae chust grab my gyurls."

Forrester turned to face Nicolson, the short fat man who employed a number of the women who worked on North Beach.

"I need to talk to Miss Morrison."

"Ye'll have tae wait," Nicolson retorted as he puffed out his chest. "She's workin'."

"I'm on police business," Forrester said, pushing the small man away. "Now piss off."

"Ye're polis?" Effie cried. "I didnae realise. Ye never said."

"Why did you ask to see me last night?" he asked. "Did Macleod put you up to it?"

Effie glanced around nervously. Their raised voices had attracted the attention of a number of other girls who craned their necks to watch the spectacle.

"We cannae talk here," she whispered and began to lead

Forrester away from the beach.

"Where d'ye think ye're goin?" Nicolson called, his round face flushed with indignation. "If ye leave I'll no' take ye back."

Forrester marched over to the rotund man and thrust a florin into his hands.

"Take this," he intoned. "It should more than cover the time I need to talk to the girl. One more sound out of you and I'll have you for obstruction. You understand?"

Nicolson pocketed the money and hurried away. Effie led Forrester away from the quayside towards the nearest pub. Once inside Forrester purchased a couple of drinks and joined the woman in the secluded booth she had chosen.

The pub was dimly lit, the thick panes of glass in the windows allowing little of the pale sunlight to filter through. The walls were stained yellow with tobacco and the glass Forrester's brandy was served in had clearly seen better days. The other patrons of the pub paid little attention to the newcomers. A couple of younger men in the corner stared at one another over their playing cards whilst the older clientèle sat hunched over the tables nursing their drinks.

Forrester handed the young woman a drink and looked at her. She removed her headscarf and allowed the waves of dark hair to fall about her face. Her brown eyes stared guiltily back at him as the colour drained from her cheeks. High cheekbones and thin lips gave her a regal look in contrast to the soiled apron and the threadbare clothes she wore. She seemed older than when he had first seen her. After their first meeting he would have guessed that she was in her early twenties, but now he would place her closer to thirty. He smiled at her in an attempt to put her at ease though it did not seem to have the desired effect. She shifted uncomfortably in her seat and reached for her drink.

"Why all the mystery?" he asked.

Effie swigged her beer thirstily and glanced around the smoky interior of the pub.

"I cannae be seen wi'ye," she whispered.

"Why not?"

"Macleod," she continued. "He said I was tae ask for ye. He wanted me tae get ye down tae the beach last night. Some of his lads had seen us talkin' an' he reckoned ye'd come if I asked."

"And you helped him." Forrester frowned. "Why? I could have been killed."

"Och, I didnae realise." She wrung her hands together as she spoke. "He offered me money an' I needed it so badly. Boabie's no' paid us the earnest-money yet an' we have tae pay for lodgings."

"Earnest money?"

"Some call it arles," she explained, "money up front for the season. When that runs low, ye're in trouble."

"Why haven't you been paid yet?"

"Boabie's a wee shite, that's why! He says he's waitin' fer the season tae begin but what he really means is he's waitin' fer the travellin' gyurls tae come so he can offer us less."

"I see," Forrester said, watching her nervous eyes dart about the room. "How much do you get for the season?"

"Twelve pound," she mumbled. "But that disnae last long when the rents are so high."

"Do you know why Jack Macphail attacked me?"

She sniffed as she shook her head and stared at the floor. With a trembling hand she pushed her hair back behind her ears.

"What can you tell me about Sruth nam Fear Gorm?" he asked.

"That's the waters between here and the Shiants."

"I know that. I also know the name means Stream of Blue Men," he continued. "What are the Blue Men?"

"Och," she smiled and the colour began to return to her cheeks, "that's chust an old tale told tae frighten bairns. The Blue Men are terrible beasties that live in the waters and sink any boats they please, but that's all nonsense. I doubt anyone really believes that."

"Can you tell me anything else about them?"

"Listen tae yerself!" she laughed. "I told ye they're no' real. My father would be able tae tell ye more, he collects the ol' stories."

"A keen reader, is he?"

"Away wi' ye," she snorted with laughter. "The old man's a crofter, he cannae read nae more than I! He's a seanchaidh, a storyteller."

"Can I meet him?" Forrester asked.

"Aye, I can take ye tae meet him, if that's what ye want. Meet me at eight o'clock tomorrow night when I finish work."

"I'd like that," he smiled. "Now, there's one more thing I need you to do."

"What's that?"

"I want you to do me a favour," he spoke calmly as he

placed three pounds on the table. "I want you to take this. The next time Macleod asks you to help, I want you to play along with him but tell me what he's up to. Do you understand?"

Effie scooped the money into her hand, her eyes glittering as she nodded her head. Forrester watched her hurry out of the pub but chose not to follow. Despite her complicity with Macleod's scheme, Forrester could not help but feel pity for the woman. She was clearly blameless of any malice towards him, her only crime being that of poverty. Moments after her departure, Colin joined him at the table.

"Well?"

"Macleod is behind it, alright," Forrester began, turning the chipped glass of brandy around in his hands. "Why he wanted me dead I don't know. What I do know is that it shows he's got something to hide and I suspect it comes in unmarked bottles."

Colin slammed his fist onto the table, the noise attracting the interest of a number of the other customers.

"Calum warned me," he cried, "he told me that I should look out fer ye."

"Calm yourself, lad," Forrester replied. "Calum doesn't need to hear about this."

They returned to North Beach where the herring girls continued their work under the watchful eye of Nicolson. A number of fishing boats had been drawn up onto the beach as their catch was unloaded.

Forrester scanned the faces until he spotted Macleod. The big man was engaged in what appeared to be a peculiarly intense exchange with an elderly gentleman who wore a peaked cap. Rowan Campbell lurked behind Macleod, puffing away on a cigarette. Macleod roared with laughter as the elderly man threw up his hands and stalked away.

"Good afternoon," Macleod sneered as Colin and Forrester approached. "How are your investigations goin'?"

"As well as can be expected," Forrester answered, ignoring the menacing looks he was receiving from Rowan Campbell.

"That old bodach," Macleod gestured to the man in the peaked cap, "wanted tae buy my fish. I tol' him that my whole catch is bought by Boabie Nicolson. He offered me a good price an' all."

"But not enough."

"I'm an honest man," Macleod said, shrugging. "I made a promise tae Boabie that all this season's catch would be his. What kind o' a man would I be if I was tae go back on my word?"

"The same kind that set one of his boys on me last night," Forrester said, his gaze not wavering from Macleod's dark eyes.

"Ha!" Macleod boomed. "D'ye think I'd be so stupid? I take it ye're referring tae the beatin' ye gave Jeck? He may work fer me but I'm no' his keeper. Jeck's got a wee problem wi' the drink an' he cannae help himself when he's got money in his pockets. When he's drunk his wages he forgets tae come tae work an' gaes out lookin' for trouble an' I'm thinkin' ye chust got in his way."

"Ye're nothin' but a god-damned liar!" Colin spat.

"Ye'd best keep that pup on a short leash, Inspector," Macleod chuckled, "he disnae have a good temper. D'ye ken that it should be me who's angry?"

"And why might that be?" Forrester asked.

"Jeck's no' goin' tae be able tae work fer at least a week. The Manannán's short o' a pair o' hands."

"Macphail attacked me, I was just defending myself."

"Aye," Macleod chuckled. "Ye did a bonny job at that. Jeck's sore bruised an' his wife reckons he may lose the sight in one eye. If ye'd defended yerself any better we'd be diggin' Jeck's grave. Now, if ye dinnae have any other questions, I'll be goin' tae talk wi' Boabie."

Both Campbell and Macleod stepped past Forrester and strolled up the beach to where Nicolson awaited them. Colin seethed with anger and Forrester held him back with a calming hand on his shoulder.

"Did ye ever hear such shite?" Colin muttered.

"He's a good liar, I'll give him that much," Forrester said. "I'll wager that even Jack Macphail would stand by that story if we were to drag him out of his sickbed and make him swear on the bible."

"What can be done?"

"Nothing," Forrester sighed. "We do nothing. We'll watch Macleod and wait for him to make the next move."

***

The streets were quiet and Forrester savoured the opportunity to be alone with his thoughts. The events of the previous evening had not come as a total surprise, he had known that sooner or later the questions he was asking would unsettle Macleod and that the fisherman would wish to silence him. What he found surprising was the lack of effort Macleod had made to distance himself from the incident. Forrester did not believe that Macphail had acted independently and the man had certainly not been under the influence of alcohol when he had attacked him. Drunk men swing wide, wild punches and are clumsy on their feet whilst Macphail had fought with the controlled poise of an experienced brawler.

Forrester hoped that the incident would not cause Colin to rush into some act of petty vengeance. Despite Forrester's initial misgivings about him, the young man had proven himself invaluable in the course of their investigations. His familiarity with the town and his ability to ingratiate himself with the locals were both useful qualities. If Colin were able to rein in his youthful impetuosity and act with a bit more circumspection, Forrester felt that he might one day make a respectable police officer.

Feeling neither tiredness nor hunger, Forrester did not hurry back to the hotel. He walked up and down the length of the harbour taking in the now familiar sights and smells of the quayside. Pausing by South Beach he leaned against a wall and gazed at the play of the moonlight on the water. He did not know what it was that caused him to look over his shoulder. Perhaps it was some primitive instinct which lies dormant in most men as Forrester was not conscious of any sound or movement that might have attracted his attention but something in his gut told him to throw a glance behind him.

Though the gas lamps of the town were lit they only illuminated the main streets. In the shadows of one of the narrow alleyways on the other side of the road stood a figure who appeared to be watching him. The figure stared at Forrester for a moment then turned and disappeared into the night.

His suspicions aroused, Forrester crossed the road and headed towards the darkened alley. He caught a second brief glimpse of the figure before it was once again swallowed up by the shadows. When he heard the quickening footsteps he knew that this was no chance encounter, someone had been watching him and wished to keep their presence a secret. Forrester could feel his pulse quickening as he began to trail the mysterious figure. Wary of another ambush by Macleod's men, he did not follow blindly but moved cautiously, keeping the figure in sight but maintaining enough distance so as not to draw any unwanted attention to himself.

Though the figure clung to the shadows and seemed to shun any well-lit streets, Forrester was certain that it was a man. He was not tall but appeared to possess unusually broad shoulders. The man's peculiar gait at first suggested to Forrester that he was inebriated but as he drew a little closer he could see that the strange manner of walking was not a drunken stagger but a pronounced limp.

The man hobbled onwards, seemingly unaware that Forrester followed him. They walked through a maze of side-streets and alleys, narrow lanes and passageways until at last they reached a courtyard at the heart of a block of tenements. The darkness was absolute and Forrester stumbled into a stack of wooden crates that toppled to the ground with a clatter. The limping man did not even pause to look at his pursuer but took to his heels and bolted through a second passage leading out of the courtyard.

Forrester swore through gritted teeth as he clambered over the debris of the crates.

"You there!" he yelled. "Come back here!"

The passageway led out onto the quayside at North Beach. Finding himself at the location of the previous night's encounter, he returned to the courtyard and armed himself with a stout piece of wood that would serve as a cudgel. This precaution was unnecessary as Forrester soon discovered that aside from a few scavenging rats the quayside was utterly deserted. Club in hand, he walked the length of the beach and searched the huge stacks of barrels for any sign of the limping man. Finding nothing, he hurled the club into the water and returned to his hotel in the foulest of moods.

Chapter 6

Effie's parents lived in a tigh dubh, a blackhouse. Forrester had difficulty hiding his surprise when they finally reached the Morrison's croft at the top of the hill at Beinn na Saighde. Compared to the more modern buildings of Stornoway and the small cottage where Calum's family dwelt, the blackhouse appeared to be a relic from the middle ages. It was a single storey dwelling of dry stone walls topped with thatch. A warm glow emanated from the small windows and a thin stream of smoke emerged from a small hole at the top of the thatch.

"It disnae look like much," Effie chuckled as she saw the expression on his face, "but it's gey comfortable inside."

Forrester stooped to follow her through the low doorway and was immediately taken aback by the pungent smell of manure. There was little light and Forrester's eyes were only able to pick out a few large shapes that stood in the shadows and snorted.

"Are those animals?" he asked.

"Aye," Effie answered. "A horse an' a coo."

Forrester was glad that the darkness masked his surprise and followed the dim form of Effie as she moved past a pile of hay to what appeared to be a wooden partition. There was the sound of a latch being lifted and then light flooded through the open doorway.

Effie's mother embraced her daughter with enthusiasm and chattered excitedly in Gaelic. Effie bore a striking resemblance to her mother, though the latter's hair was streaked with grey and her face was lined with the cares of old age. Her father, a tall man with a long tangled beard, rose to his feet and planted a kiss on his daughter's cheek. He looked inquisitively at Forrester and stepped forward with his hand extended.

"Dè an t-ainm a tha oirbh?" he asked.

"This is Edmund Forrester, father," Effie interjected, seeing Forrester's confusion. "He wishes to hear some of your stories but he disnae have the Gaelic."

"Very well," the old man smiled genially and shook Forrester's hand with a firm grip. "I only hope my English is no' too rough for ye. Did ye walk here? Come an' have a seat, ye must be tired."

"Thank you, Mister Morrison," Forrester said as he was led to the long wooden bench that took up most of one side of the room.

"Och, the English're so well-mannered!" Effie's mother laughed. "Call him Angus, dear... Ye can call me Caitlin."

The room was lit by a number of lanterns that hung from the low timbers of the roof. A peat fire burned in the centre of the stone floor, its fragrant smoke masking the smell of the livestock past the partition wall. A black cauldron hung from a chain above the fire and Caitlin stirred its contents with a long wooden spoon.

"If I'd known we'd have visitors I'd have prepared something more substantial than broth," the old woman commented. "I hope that suits ye both."

"Ye shouldnae trouble yourself, mother," Effie responded. "Broth will suit us chust fine."

Angus Morrison opened one of the small cupboards on the opposite wall and removed four small glasses and a dusty bottle.

"This is a fine malt. Twenty years old," he said proudly. "My brother brought this back wi' him the last time he went tae Glasgow."

Forrester watched Angus fill the glasses with generous measures and accepted the glass with a smile. Angus pulled up a squat stool and sat on it so that his back was warmed by the glowing fire. Though by no means a young man, Effie's father seemed carved out of wood. His broad shoulders and muscular arms suggested a rugged life of strenuous work.

"Slàinte!" he raised his glass before taking a mouthful of his drink and stretching out his legs.

"Edmund is interested in the Blue Men," Effie said.

"There's many a tale about them," Angus said, stroking his chin thoughtfully. "What would ye like tae know?"

"What can you tell me?"

"They're no' mermaids, nor selkies, nor kelpies... Too many folks get their tales mixed up in the tellin'. The Blue Men are a Clan, like the Macleods or the Mackenzies, but they live under the waters o' the Minch an' take little interest in the affairs of the Hielanders. The only time they show themselves is when man intrudes on their territory... the Sound of Shiant or Sruth nam Fear Gorm. The waters used tae be known as the current

- 88 -

o' destruction an' it's had a bad reputation for as long as anyone cares tae remember."

"Are they men?" Forrester asked.

"In a manner o' speakin'," Angus replied, "but not such as you or I. They can breathe underwater like fish an' have long strong arms for swimmin'. Their skin is blue – as yours would be if ye had tae swim in the Minch all day long. Any boat they see crossin' their waters they swim up tae. Their chief will offer a rhyme in Gaelic an' if the Captain o' the ship cannae answer with a rhyme quick enough, or disnae have the Gaelic, then the Blue Men swim aroun' the boat and whip the waters intae a storm. They're said tae sink the ships an' feast on the flesh o' the drowned."

"Where can I find them?"

"Find them?" the old man wheezed with laughter. "Ye cannae find them! They're no' real! It is chust a story told by sailors tae frighten children. Ye might as well try an' fish for the salmon o' knowledge! Now it's said that they live around the Charmed Isles... the Shiants... but all you'll find there is Big Donald Campbell an' his family."

"Enough of this," Caitlin interrupted. "Can ye no' tell a nicer story tonight, Angus? Ye ken full well how I hate tae hear those nasty old tales. D'ye remember the nightmares Effie used tae have as a bairn?"

Angus shrugged his vast shoulders ruefully and drained the remainder of the whisky from his glass.

"I was chust tellin' the Englishman what he wanted tae hear," he grumbled, "it wasnae me who made up that tale so I shouldnae be held responsible."

"Ye can make yerself useful an' cut the bread," Caitlin scolded.

Forrester watched hungrily as Caitlin spooned out bowlfuls of the steaming soup. Angus handed him a chunk of crusty bread and after saying a brief grace, the family began eating. The soup contained vegetables and small pieces of stewed mutton. Forrester emptied his bowl quickly and gratefully accepted a second helping.

"What brings ye tae the islands then?" Caitlin asked.

"I'm investigating the disappearance of Alistair Mackinnon," Forrester stated.

"Calum's boy?" Angus asked. "He should never have let his son off the croft. What business did the lad have messin' in boats?"

"It's a shame," Caitlin sighed, "it seems like only yesterday he was learnin' tae walk. He was a bonnie wee thing."

"If ye're investigatin' Ali Mackinnon's death," Angus said, "why're ye askin' about Sruth nam Fear Gorm? Dinnae tell me ye think the Blue Men did it!"

Forrester joined in the family as they laughed and shook his head.

"No," he answered. "It is nothing as outlandish as that, I'm afraid."

"He's been talkin' tae Murdo Macleod," Effie said as she refilled their glasses with whisky.

"Macleod?" Angus scowled. "There's a man ye cannae trust. Only last year him an' his boys hired themselves out tae help the factors clear the crofters off the mainland. A man that'll dae that would dae anythin' for money."

"He seems to have a lot of influence over people," Forrester commented.

"Influence?" Angus snorted derisively. "It's fear. People are afraid of Murdo Macleod. He's got muscle in the strong arm o' his boys an' he's got money behind him. A man wi' power an' money can dae whatsoever he pleases. I heard that he gave Kenny Maciver the thrashin' o' his life chust for leanin' on that blasted boat o' his. Poor Kenny was spittin' teeth for days after but the Sheriff wouldnae touch Macleod for fear o' reprisals. But I see from your face that ye're a man no' afraid tae fight back. I hope the other fellow came off worse."

Forrester's hand moved self-consciously to his flattened nose. "I came by this a long time ago," he mumbled.

"Och, I didnae mean tae offend ye," Angus apologised. "They say it's the marks that make a man."

"I understand Macleod has also claimed fishing rights on a large stretch of the Minch," Forrester attempted to steer the conversation back to more important matters.

"That's true," Effie said. "The other boats that launch from Stornoway daren't sail past Loch Odhairn for fear of crossin' paths wi' Macleod. With so many boats sailin' from Ness it's gettin' gey crowded out on the waters an' the catches are gettin' smaller. It's no' fair when Macleod's boats have the whole Sound o' Shiant tae themselves."

"Terrible," Caitlin tutted and began to tidy away the dinner things. "Small wonder so many're flittin' overseas."

"Hush now. We're no' leavin' the island an' that's final," Angus grunted.

Forrester gazed at the smouldering peat fire and took a swig of the whisky. The smoke drifted lazily up into the rafters of the house, leaving only its distinctive aroma. What Angus Morrison had told him about the Blue Men was interesting but could hardly be seen as significant. His investigation had to remain focused on reality, not on folklore. He had learned a little more about Murdo Macleod and liked the man even less as a consequence. Taking another mouthful, he considered the possibility that Macleod was using the stories of the Blue Men to deter the other fishermen from entering the Sound of Shiant in order to continue his whisky smuggling undisturbed. He quickly dismissed this scenario; Macleod did not need to rely on folktales to scare people who were already afraid of him and the majority of people he encountered were aware of the smuggled whisky so there seemed little need for such caution. There was something else about the Sound of Shiant which Macleod wanted to keep secret.

The small carriage clock that sat on the dresser chimed eleven and Effie rose to her feet.

"We must be goin'," she said. "It'll take us the best part of an hour tae walk home an' tomorrow is the Sabbath."

"Ye can stay if ye want. We still have your old bed made up chust in case." Caitlin drew back a pair of curtains that Forrester had taken for a cupboard to reveal a small space set in the panelling that contained a few pillows and a tweed blanket.

"I wish I could, mother," Effie said as she kissed her cheeks, "but Mister Forrester will get me home safe, won't ye?"

They bade the elderly couple farewell and stepped out into the cold night. A strong gust lifted the bottom of Effie's skirts and she giggled as she held them down.

"A fine Scottish breeze," Forrester joked as he saw her embarrassment.

Buffeted by the wind, they walked side by side down the hill. They headed in the direction of Stornoway, its lights winking in the darkness. A light rain began to spit and Forrester felt Effie slip her arm into his.

"I'm cold," she said. "It always seems so much worse goin' back intae town."

Forrester said nothing but smiled, enjoying the sensation of feeling a woman close by him. It had been so long since he had experienced such close proximity to a female that he was left feeling slightly giddy.

"D'ye like the island?" she asked after a few moments of comfortable silence.

"Yes," he replied. "It's so different to what I'm used to."

"Different?"

"Everything moves at a different pace."

"Ye mean it's borin'," she retorted.

"Far from it," he continued, "in the few days I've been here I've been out on a fishing boat, drunk my body-weight in Scotch, listened to tall tales of sea-monsters and been assaulted by a man who didn't speak a word of English. If anything, Lewis keeps a man on his toes."

She laughed and squeezed his arm.

"Have ye forgiven me for that?"

"What's there to forgive?" he asked. "You needed money and Macleod took advantage of your situation. I don't think you had any choice in the matter."

"That's no' true." She pulled away from him and folded her arms across her chest. "I could've told Murdo Macleod to go hang himself, but I didnae. Ye'd shown me nothin' but kindness and I helped him near kill ye."

"It takes more than that to kill me," he said soothingly. "And you? Do you like living on the island?"

"When I was younger I didnae mind it so much," she groaned, "but I dinnae ken how much more of it I can stand. Aside from a visit tae Ullapool when I was fourteen, I've never left the island. As I've grown bigger, it seems tae have grown smaller. Everyone's aware of everyone else's business and I cannae move fer bumpin' intae a cousin or someone askin' after mother an' father. I just want tae go tae a big city where I can be a stranger an' get on by myself."

"You'd miss nothing?"

"What's there tae miss? The rate they're pullin' herrin' out the Minch there'll be none left. Besides which, I'd be happy never tae see another herrin' as long as I live. There's nae future here. I chust want tae get away from the Boabie Nicolsons and the Murdo Macleods o' this world. They're takin' everythin' an' puttin' nothin' back."

"What about your family?"

"Ye heard mother talk o' flittin'. Father disnae want tae leave but life is gettin' harder for crofters an' he's no' a young man anymore. If the factors were tae come a-knockin' I'd wager they'd pack up their things an' follow mother's cousins tae Quebec. But listen tae me goin' on like this... Tell me about yerself."

"There's not much to say, really," Forrester thrust his hands deeper into the pockets of his greatcoat. "I'm just a simple policeman."

"Ye're modest," she chided. "Are y' married?"

"Once. I was married, but now divorced."

"Why did ye leave her?"

Forrester shook his head and chewed on his bottom lip.

"I didn't," he said. "She left me."

"Whatever for?"

"It was complicated," he sighed, wishing that she would talk about anything else.

"How?" she pressed him.

"I was preoccupied with my work. I let it get in the way of the relationship."

"That's no' complicated," she said, "it's stupid."

"Perhaps," he answered vaguely.

"Are ye goin' tae marry again?"

"That's pretty unlikely. I'm afraid my days of wine and roses have passed. People take one look at my face and all they see is the nose. Most just assume I'm some kind of bruiser."

"I don't."

Forrester stopped and turned to face Effie. Though the night was dark, the pale moonlight lit her face and her eyes glittered as they looked up at him.

"Oh, really?" he asked. "What do you see when you look at me?"

"Strength," she replied quickly, "and stability. Ye're no' a man who'd run off an' leave a gyurl. Ye'd look after her."

She slipped her hand into his and clung to him as they continued their walk.

"Ye can leave at any time," she said after a while. "Ye ken?"

"Why would I leave?"

"I don't trust Macleod," she said as her hold on his arm grew tighter. "He wouldnae think twice of killin' ye."

"I don't trust him either," he said, "but I have to find out if he's responsible for the death of young Alistair Mackinnon."

"If ye knew he was, if ye had evidence... would ye leave then?"

"Once I saw the guilty party prosecuted, yes."

"Why does it matter to ye? Why d'ye care about the fate of a boy ye never met an' never will?"

"It's my job," he answered. "Someone has to care."

She stopped and took both of his hands in hers. He could see her eyes welling with tears and felt her tremble.

"Ye're in danger," she said. "I want ye tae leave tomorrow. I cannae tell ye more but I dinnae want tae see ye get hurt."

"Macleod can try," he intoned, "but he won't be able to hurt me."

"It's not Macleod I'm afraid of," she shuddered. "He has powerful friends."

Forrester pulled his hands clear and rummaged in the deep pocket of his greatcoat. Effie gasped as she saw the moonlight glint off the black steel of the Webley revolver.

He smiled. "So do I."

***

Colin gazed into the speckled surface of the old mirror and adjusted his tie. Satisfied that it was straight, he set about running a comb through his hair in an attempt to tame the unruly curls. Having decided that he would spend the evening in the town, he had spent over an hour bathing, shaving and dressing. The brass tub he had bathed in sat before the fire and was now occupied by young Heather who sang to herself as she splashed in the warm water. Maggie Mackinnon patted her daughter on the head and smiled before handing Colin his third cup of tea of the evening.

"What d'ye look like?" she chuckled. "Ye're a long ways from Sauchiehall Street!"

"Aye, well," he shrugged, "but that shouldnae stop a man from makin' an effort. This here is my best suit."

Maggie helped him into the jacket of his suit and brushed a few stray hairs from his shoulders.

"Is this what the men are wearin' in the cities then?"

"They are. Those that can afford it."

"That's cut from a fine cloth, Colin. I daresay it cost a lot."

"Ye're no' wrong, Maggie. A friend o' mine is a tailor an' he gave me a fair price. Even so, I'll still be payin' this one back for some time yet."

Calum Mackinnon slapped the arms of his comfortable chair and roared with laughter.

"An' who d'ye think ye'll be impressin' in that? The gyurls o' the island aren't so taken wi' such finery."

Colin splashed cologne on his cheeks before turning to face his older cousin.

"That shows how little ye ken of the fairer sex, Calum," he smirked. "These island gyurls might be content tae marry a hairy crofter wi' dirt under his nails such as yerself, but they all dream o' bein' swept off their feet by a well-dressed gent. Ye're chust jealous 'cause the only time ye'll wear a suit like this is when ye're bein' buried!"

"That'll be one time too many!"

Colin turned back to continue admiring his reflection in the mirror. After numerous minute adjustments to his hair, he picked up his cup of tea and sipped it.

"Will ye no' eat a thing before goin'?" Maggie asked.

"Aye, Maggie's right," Calum said, nodding. "If ye're fixin' on drinkin' ye should eat some crowdie an' biscuits. It'll soak up the whisky."

"Thank you, no. I'm late already. I wouldnae want tae keep the gyurls waitin'?"

"And who's the lucky gyurl ye're meetin' with?"

"All of 'em." Colin winked and lit the cigarette that dangled from his lips.

The walk to town took Colin a little longer than normal as he took great care to avoid walking near the muddy puddles that covered the roads. He breathed a sigh of relief when he finally reached the pavements of Cromwell Street and was able to quicken his pace. As predicted, his fashionable attire attracted the right amount of interest from the locals. Men shook their heads and muttered under their breath as he sauntered by, but he paid them little attention. The young women raised their eyebrows and giggled as he tipped his hat and flashed them his most sophisticated smile. He walked with a spring in his step, every smile he received from one of the women further bolstering his ego. When he reached the pub, he spent a moment checking his reflection in the window before pushing open the doors with a theatrical flourish and stepping inside.

He placed his hat beside him at the bar and caught the landlord's attention. He ordered a whisky and water and leaned back to survey the other drinkers. His arrival had not gone unnoticed and he felt a strange satisfaction as he felt a dozen pairs of eyes upon him. He smiled and sipped his drink, noting with some pleasure that he was the best dressed man in the bar.

It was not long before a group of curious locals had beckoned the outlandishly dressed stranger over to their table and he was regaling them with exaggerated tales of city life. Most worked on the fishing boats and a few recognised him from the harbour.

"What brings ye tae the island?" a heavily bearded man asked as he handed Colin another glass of whisky.

"I'm helping the police out with an investigation."

"The Englishman wi' the busted nose? "

"That's him. Don't judge him by his appearance; the man's mind is razor sharp. Problem is, the case wasn't one his superiors thought he could handle on his own, so they asked me tae accompany him."

"Are ye a policeman an' all?" asked a fair haired young woman who sat beside Colin.

Colin shook his head and smiled. "Me? No. I'm more of a special assistant they call in tae gi' a hand when things look a bit much for chust one man. Ye'd be surprised how much demand there is for my services."

"I hear the Englishman was askin' about young Ali Mackinnon."

Colin smiled cryptically and took a mouthful from his glass.

"That's a private police matter. I couldnae comment.

However, if ye'd be willin' tae stand me another wee dram I'd be more'n happy tae tell ye about the case of the Clydebank strangler..."

The evening wore on and Colin's accounts of his imaginary victories grew wilder and wilder. A crowd had gathered around the table to hear his stories and the drinks were flowing freely. Colin was pleased with himself. He had not had to reach into his pocket to pay for a single drink for over an hour and the locals roared with delight as he spun another yarn about the seedy and largely fictitious Glasgow underworld.

"Ye have tae understand that Mad Murray Martin was a dangerous man an' I'm no' ashamed tae admit that I was frightened for my life when he stepped out o' the shadows..."

It was not just the crowd around the table who listened attentively to the young man's tall tales. Rowan Campbell stood hunched over the bar, an untouched bottle of beer before him. He smoked incessantly as he listened to Colin's account of how he single-handedly wrestled yet another dangerous crook into submission. When the story was finished Campbell dropped a couple of coins onto the bar, slipped quietly from the pub and hurried over to North Beach.

"Are ye sure of it?" Macleod frowned.

Campbell nodded.

"He's the cove that was with the Englishman. You should hear the way he's carryin' on. If half of what he says is true then we should be wary of him. The Englishman is already sniffin' around more'n I care tae see."

Macleod finished coiling a tarred rope about his arms and tossed it into one of the boats. He ran a hand through his thick beard and gazed at the reflection of the moonlight on the water.

"Let me worry about the Englishman. Perhaps we ought tae

have a wee chat wi' his young friend."

Macleod stuck his fingers in his mouth and whistled at a young woman who was helping mend the nets. She looked up from her work and Macleod beckoned her over with a tilt of his head.

"Aye, Murdo?"

"How would ye like tae earn yerself a few easy pennies?" Macleod asked.

"That depends on what ye're askin' me tae dae."

"I'll no' lie tae ye, Mary. Ye're a pretty gyurl an' I want ye tae use that pretty face tae make a new friend."

"I'm no' a whore," she said indignantly and turned to leave.

Macleod's arms shot out and grabbed hold of her shoulder. He exerted a little pressure with his large hands and turned her back to face him.

"We all ken ye're in need of the money since your hands are nae good for guttin' herring. I'm no' askin' ye tae lay wi' him," he intoned. "I chust want ye tae bring him out here so me an' the lads can have a quiet word."

"Who is he?"

"Ye'll find him in the Star. A stuck-up young cove from the mainland. Dressed up like a damned peacock an' squawkin' chust as much. Let him buy ye a dram or two an' then see if he wants tae walk ye home. Bring him this way, an' we'll do the rest."

***

Colin did not once question the motives of the attractive fair-haired girl who sat beside him and pressed her warm body against his. She clutched his arm and smiled sweetly as he spoke about himself and laughed at all his jokes, regardless of whether she understood them or not.

Colin's head swam with drink and when Mary asked him if he'd like to go for a walk outside, he winked lasciviously and offered her his arm.

Mary pressed herself close to him as they walked away from the pub. The night was cold and he put an arm around her when he felt her begin to shiver. Colin chattered aimlessly for a while, his questions and inane comments receiving little or no response. They walked on in silence, the sound of their footsteps on the cobbles echoing about the quiet streets.

As they reached the narrow stairs that led down to North Beach, Mary tugged his arm and they began to descend.

"Why're we goin' down here?" he asked.

"The boats," she replied. "We'll be alone there."

He chuckled and followed eagerly. At the bottom of the steps, he reached out and pulled her close to him, pressing his lips against hers. She wrenched herself free and slapped him hard across the cheek before sprinting back up the steps to Cromwell Street. Colin made a move to follow her but a familiar voice stopped him.

"That's a fine suit ye're wearin'."

Murdo Macleod stepped out of the shadows and strode towards him. He struck a match off the rough brick wall, cupped the flame in his hands and lit a cigarette. Having tossed the spent match aside, the glowing tip of the cigarette was the sole illumination in the oppressive darkness.

"What d'ye want?" Colin slurred.

"Me? I'm a simple man, I dinnae want for much. I'm more interested what it is ye're wantin' of me."

"I don't understand."

"D'ye no'? First I hear that ye've been askin' tae be taken out tae the Shiants an' askin' questions about my whisky. Then ye call me a liar in front o' my boys, an' now I hear ye're tellin' all o' Stornoway that ye're some damned hero fixin' tae arrest me."

"It's just talk," Colin stammered, his mouth feeling unnaturally dry.

"Careless talk can be dangerous," Macleod answered solemnly. "I've got a reputation tae uphold on this island. I'm chust hopin' that folks have more sense than tae listen tae such shite."

"I meant nothin' by it."

"Ye shouldnae lie tae me, boy. Can ye no' see that I have tae teach ye a lesson?"

Macleod's ominous threat left Colin in a paroxysm of fear. The confidence given to him by the alcohol vanished and was replaced with the dreadful anticipation of what Macleod might do to him. Sobered by these thoughts, Colin muttered a clumsy apology and stumbled towards the steps in order that he might retreat to the relative safety of the town. A figure swaggered down the steps and stood blocking his way. Colin began to tremble as he met Rowan Campbell's dark gaze and realised that he was trapped.

"Get in the boat," Macleod snarled.

Without uttering a word, Colin did as he was told.

Chapter 7

Forrester awoke with a start and looked dazedly around the room. The sharp hammering that had interrupted his dream continued. His bleary eyes were drawn towards the door that shook on its hinges with the pounding.

He groaned as he crawled from the warmth of his bed and tiptoed on bare feet across the cold floor to the door. Calum stood on the other side, his face ashen and visibly shaken.

"Ye have tae come," he said breathlessly. "There's been an accident o' some kind."

"What do you mean?" Forrester asked as he pulled on his clothes.

"It's Colin," Calum's voice shook as he spoke. "He's dead."

"Dead?"

Calum nodded and Forrester saw the tears glistening in the large man's beard.

"Drowned," he mumbled. "He was found floatin' in the waters out by the mouth o' the bay chust after dawn. I came here as soon as I heard."

Having dressed, Forrester followed Calum down Cromwell Street to North Beach. Despite being the Sabbath, the news of the death had travelled fast and already there was a large crowd of people assembled by the quayside. Forrester barged through their midst until he stood before the grey tweed blanket that lay covering the body. Only the pointed toe of Colin's fashionable boots protruded from beneath the makeshift shroud and Forrester recognised them immediately. He pulled the blanket back and glimpsed at the pallid face and the blank staring eyes before covering the body once more.

"Get these people out of here," he growled, "and get me the Sheriff."

***

The body was taken to the house of Doctor Roderick Murray who lived a short distance from the church Forrester had attended the previous Sunday. It had not been easy to rouse the doctor from his bed and the old man had complained about working on the Sabbath. Murray had proven a little more amenable when Forrester threatened to leave the dead body on the front step of the house until Monday. The white haired physician had muttered ominously to himself as he conducted a cursory examination of the deceased but did not engage in any form of conversation. Forrester paced the room and smoked as he watched the elderly doctor pick up a pen and begin writing his report.

Like the doctor, the Sheriff had not been best pleased to be summoned to work on a Sunday. Forrester noted the relief on the man's face as he made his introductions and presented his credentials. The Sheriff was more than happy to abdicate all responsibility to the Englishman and departed in haste, leaving Forrester alone in the study of the doctor.

"Cause of death," Murray spoke aloud as he wrote, "drowning."

"Do you have any idea how he came to be out there?" Forrester asked.

"Friend of yours, was he?" Murray signed his name with name with a flourish and then peered over the thin frame of his spectacles.

"He was supposed to be looking after me."

"You look as though you can take care of yourself," the doctor replied.

"What happened?"

"My guess would be that he didn't go swimming, unless your young friend was in the habit of swimming fully clothed."

Forrester said nothing and the doctor took his cue to continue.

"I would say that he was out in a boat of some kind and fell into the water."

"How far out was he?"

"Hard to tell," the doctor sighed as he removed his glasses. "He's been in the water all night, that much is clear. But with the tides around here it is impossible to tell where he could have fallen in."

Forrester wandered over to the table where the body lay and began his own examination.

"As far as I knew, Colin had no intention of going out in a

boat," he muttered. "Besides which, he wouldn't have gone without me."

"Inspector Forrester," the doctor spoke indignantly, "I have worked for many years on this island and have seen more than my fair share of drowned men. There is no mystery as to how this man died. It is not uncommon for young men who have drunk too much to fall in the water and drown. I see two or three similar cases every year."

Ignoring the elderly man's protestations, Forrester lifted Colin's head and crouched in order to look at the underside of it.

"There's something here," he said as he pushed a tangle of hair aside. "A bruise."

"A bruise?" the doctor approached to look at the mark Forrester indicated. "Ah yes, there is a contusion of some kind..."

"Any suggestions on how it came to be there?"

"There could be a multitude of reasons," the doctor said, waving a dismissive hand. "That could have been the point at which he fell into the water or he could have been struck by the boom... That certainly would account for his drowning. To be honest, the bruise may well have nothing to do with the young man's death. I'm not in the habit of speculating on such matters."

Sensing that Murray was going to be of no help, Forrester gave a noncommittal grunt and pressed his fingers against the bruise. The fracture yielded to the pressure but he gave no indication of his discovery to the doctor.

"You're probably correct," he said and rose to his feet. "I will make arrangements with the family for the burial."

Forrester stepped into the adjoining room where Calum had been waiting for the previous hour. Though still in shock, some of the colour had returned to the man's ruddy cheeks and he managed a smile when he saw Forrester approach.

"What news?" he asked.

"We shouldn't speak here," Forrester said, taking him by the arm and leading him to the door. "I think we're both in need of a drink."

***

Calum drained his third glass of Scotch and slammed the glass onto the table with such force that Forrester was surprised it did not crack. All traces of grief had vanished from his face, to be replaced by a simmering rage that transformed the Scotsman's demeanour. He sat with clenched fists and scowled as he listened to Forrester's account of the post-mortem.

"It sounds tae me that Murray is hidin' something from us," he seethed.

"He could be," Forrester agreed, "or he could simply be incompetent. Either way, there is something suspicious about the injury on Colin's head."

"A swingin' boom can dae that tae a man," Maggie said and placed a calming hand on her husband's shoulder.

"So can a blackjack," Forrester stated plainly. "I've seen dozens of wounds just like that. A sharp blow to the back of the head with a sap can knock a man unconscious. Drop the body in the water and the poor soul drowns. Such wounds can easily be explained away and it looks like an accident."

"Macleod," Calum roared, "I'll kill him."

"You'll do no such thing," Forrester snapped, "unless you want to find yourself dancing at Gallows Hill."

The raised voices of the men disturbed the Mackinnons' young daughter, who began to wail in her crib. Maggie plucked up the child and held her close.

"Hush now, Heather," she cooed to the girl as she glared angrily at the men, "there's nothin' tae fear."

"I trust you'll make arrangements for the funeral, Calum," Forrester said as he shrugged on his greatcoat.

Calum nodded and showed him to the door. The afternoon sun was hidden behind a swathe of grey clouds from which a light drizzle fell. Forrester buttoned up his coat and stuffed his hands deep into his pockets. The walk back to Stornoway was not far but he walked briskly, his eyes fixed on the ground before him and his mind occupied with thoughts of what could have happened the night before.

He had spent the previous day around the town in Colin's company. Their attempts to gather information about Murdo Macleod had been unsuccessful and Forrester had been glad when his companion grew irritated with their lack of progress and returned to the Mackinnons' house. As arranged, Forrester had met with Effie at eight o'clock and gone to visit her parents. Less than twelve hours later, Colin's body is found floating at the mouth of the bay. Was Macleod behind his death? If it was an accident, the timing could not have been worse. Forrester himself had been attacked by one of Macleod's men two days before but without any firm evidence he was unable to accuse the fisherman of foul play.

The light rain turned heavier and Forrester swore under his breath whilst quickening his pace. By the time he reached his hotel he was soaked to the skin and collapsed into one of the armchairs in the lounge with an audible squelch. He ran a hand through his sodden hair and shuddered when he felt the water trickle down the back of his neck. His discomfort was added to when a couple of elderly men who he had seen propping up the bar on previous evenings broke into tuneless, vociferous song:

It fell upon a Wednesday
Brown Robyn's men went tae sea,
But they saw neither moon nor sun,
Nor starlight with their ee.

We'll cast kevels us amang,
See wha the unhappy man may be;
The kevel fell on Brown Robyn,
The master-man was he.

The two old men grinned with mirth as the door to the lounge swung open and a short man with a prominent hunched back staggered in carrying a large leather case. They beckoned him over and he flipped the catches on his case and lifted an old battered accordion from within. With a twisted smile, the hunchback strapped the cumbersome instrument to his chest and accompanied the old men's song with an equally discordant melody.

It is nae wonder, said Brown Robyn
Altho I dinnae thrive,
For wi' my mother I had twa bairns,
And wi' my sister five.

So tie me tae a plank o' wood,
An' throw me in the sea;
An' if I sink, ye may bid me sink,

But if I swim, chust lat me be.

They've tied him tae a plank o' wood,
And thrown him in the sea;
He didnae sink tho they bade him sink,
He swam and they lat him be.

The song finished and Forrester breathed a sigh of relief. He watched as the hunchback and the old men moved around the room with their hats in their hands. The hunchback shuffled over to where he sat and thrust a threadbare tweed cap under his nose.

"I'll give you a ha'penny if you promise not to play anything else," Forrester grumbled.

"He's no' the first tae say that." The hunchback smiled and eased himself into the opposite chair. "Is he no' a music lover, then?"

"I like music," Forrester retorted, "but I was hard-pushed to hear a tune amidst that dreadful noise."

"Sure!" The hunchback threw his head as far back as it would go and laughed. "He's no' afraid o' speakin' his mind is he? What's he called?"

"I beg your pardon?"

"His name?" The hunchback chuckled and patted himself on the chest. "This fine form they call Jonah Macaskill but what dae they call him?"

"Edmund Forrester. Now, leave me alone."

"An' Englishman, he is," the hunchback continued, "very far from his city he is. What brings him tae the long island? Is he enjoyin' the fine weather?"

Forrester looked at the man who called himself Jonah and wondered whether he was being made fun of. The hunchback was not old, in his late twenties at the most and dressed in an ill-fitting suit of rough wool. His head was covered with a mess of unruly hair that stuck out at all angles and added to his bizarre appearance. The deformity on his back was such that he did not appear to possess a neck and he walked with a shuffle that one would expect of a much older man. One leg appeared to be longer than the other and he wore a block of wood strapped to the bottom of the boot on his shorter leg to compensate for the difference. Pale blue eyes glittered from beneath the fringe of shaggy hair and Forrester shifted uncomfortably under their gaze.

"I'm here on business," he muttered. "And the weather is bloody horrible."

Jonah clapped his hands with glee and rocked back and forth in his seat with laughter.

"Och, this is fine spring weather, he'll no' find rain so clean anywhere else in Britain. I'll wager he's the sort who'd complain even in sunshine. There's nae pleasin' some folks, especially the English."

"I was perfectly content until you came along."

"He's angry, this one," Jonah said gleefully. "Perhaps he misses his friend."

"What did you say?"

"The friend he lost," Jonah continued. "He should be more careful."

"Now listen here." Forrester reached across the table and grabbed the hunchback by the collar. "What are you getting at? What do you know about Colin's death?"

"We didnae ken his friend but we're wise enough no' tae meddle wi' the business o' Murdo Macleod."

"How do you know Macleod has anything to do with Colin's death?" Forrester tightened his grip on the Jonah's collar. "Speak now, before I wring what little neck you have."

"Oh ho!" Jonah grinned as his face grew redder and his voice began to croak. "He's gey angry he is. But he disnae understand that Jonah is no friend of Macleod and ol' Murdo Macleod cannae stand the sight of Jonah. We only wanted tae help him, but if he wishes tae choke a poor old cripple, then choke away..."

Forrester released the hunchback and dropped him back into his seat.

"You were the one following me on Friday night, weren't you? What do you want from me?"

Jonah straightened his collar and smacked his lips noisily.

"Thirsty work, makin' new friends, is it not? Perhaps he'd buy Jonah a wee dram and then they can discuss all this mischief in the Minch. Perhaps Jonah could take him out there in a boat?"

Forrester wandered over to the bar and ordered a whisky for Jonah and a large glass of water for himself. As the landlady handed him the drinks she leaned over to him and whispered conspiratorially.

"Buy a drink for poor Crotach by any means, but ye dinnae listen tae a word he says. He's as mad as he is ugly."

Forrester thanked the woman and returned to his seat. The hunchback reached for his drink and slurped it thirstily. Jonah drained half the glass in a few swallows before wiping his mouth with the back of his hand.

"The water o' life," he beamed. "Will he no' hae a wee drink wi' Jonah?"

"The water will be enough for me. I've had enough Scotch in the past few days to last me a lifetime."

"That depends on how long he goes on livin'. If he plans tae go up 'gainst the friends of Macleod, he might ne'er taste another drop."

"What do you mean?" Forrester frowned. "Have you been talking to Macleod?"

Jonah shook his head and pushed his unruly hair away from his eyes.

"Macleod disnae talk tae Jonah. He wouldnae pay a farthin' tae see him dancin' in a freakshow."

"What can you tell me of Macleod? Who are these friends of his you mentioned?"

"Questions! Questions! Always questions!" Jonah emptied his glass and pushed it across the table to Forrester. "Such thirsty work."

"No." Forrester pushed the glass back at the hunchback. "First you tell me about Macleod and then I'll think about buying you another drink."

"He is interested, isn't he? Macleod has many friends but there are some he is ashamed of. Those friends he wouldnae meet in town. There's a bay out past Arnish Point where they sometimes meet on a Monday. Jonah sees them but disnae let them see him."

"Who are they?" Forrester asked.

"Men of the sea," Jonah replied.

"What do you mean? Pirates? Smugglers?"

Jonah whooped with laughter and slapped his thigh. He looked around the lounge and, once satisfied that nobody was eavesdropping on their conversation, continued.

"The Englishman wouldnae understand unless Jonah shows him."

"You'll take me out there in a boat?"

Jonah shook his head and smiled cryptically.

"But you said that we could go out there in a boat," Forrester continued.

"Jonah said he could take him across the Minch but he disnae have a boat. We'll walk. Tomorrow night we'll take a bottle o' whisky an' go stand watch."

"Why should I trust you?"

"Who else can he trust?"

Jonah grasped Forrester's hand and clenched it firmly.

"Until tomorrow." The hunchback smiled then hoisted the case containing his accordion and shuffled out of the room.

Forrester returned to the bar and ordered another glass of water.

"He's a poor soul, that Crotach," the landlady sighed. "Ye're a kind man tae share a drink wi' him."

"Why do you call him Crotach?"

"Few folks call him Jonah," she sniffed. "Crotach means hunchback."

"What can you tell me about him?"

"Och, I could tell ye chust about everythin' about everyone on the island, had ye the time tae listen. I think he grew up near

Loch Orasaigh, or so I've heard. As ye might've guessed, he disnae work as such but lives by the charity o' folk such as yourself. He didnae used tae talk such rot but a few years back he lost his mother, God rest her soul, an' the boy's mind went wi' her."

"You think he's mad?"

"There's none stranger in Stornoway. Some folks daen't even gi' him the time o' day for fear he'll start babblin' at them."

"Such as Murdo Macleod?"

The landlady fell silent and looked away. She picked up an empty glass and rubbed it vigorously with a cloth.

"Ye'd best cross yerself if ye're thinkin' of mentionin' Macleod's name so casual. There's more'n a few who drink in here that work fer him an' in a wee town nothin' travels faster than careless words."

"Am I supposed to be afraid of the man?"

"Och no," the landlady said, rolling her eyes. "Ye can leave this place any time ye want an' return tae your big city. Those who have tae live here an' scratch out a livin', they're the ones who're right tae be afeared. A man as influential an' powerful as Macleod is no' tae be underestimated."

"Jonah mentioned Macleod's friends out by Arnish Point. Does that mean anything to you?"

"Should it? I'm sure a man such as Macleod has friends all over the island an' on the mainland. But as I've said, be wary of payin' too much attention tae what Crotach tells ye."

Forrester returned to his seat. He considered what the landlady had told him as he sipped his water but found his mind wandering back to what the hunchback had told him about Macleod and his mysterious friends. There was something about Jonah, something peculiar yet trustworthy. He decided that it would be worth following the hunchback out to the bay to investigate whether there was any truth in his words. Though a slim chance, he hoped that by discovering the identity of Macleod's mysterious friends, he might be able to shed some light on Colin's death.

Chapter 8

Forrester allowed himself to drop onto the heather and sighed with relief as he sank into its soft embrace. The walk from Stornoway had taken several hours. Despite his obvious infirmities, Jonah had led the way, marching across miles of peat bogs, bare rocks and heather. Forrester struggled to keep up, ill at ease with the water-logged terrain of Arnish moor.

He would curse when his feet got tangled in bracken or when he found himself sinking up to his ankles in rank puddles. Such outbursts would bring about a sharp word from Jonah or a hiss of warning, although the hunchback never once slowed his pace.

"Has he ne'er taken a walk before?" Jonah chuckled.

"There is a bloody big difference between a walk," Forrester complained breathlessly and waved a hand at the moon hanging in the darkness above them, "and a midnight march through a swamp."

"A swamp?" Jonah asked. "There's few things more beauteous than a moonlit moor."

"This had best be worthwhile." Forrester scowled as he extricated his foot from the cloying mud.

"No' far the now, Englishman. He'll see soon enough."

They walked in silence for another ten minutes, the only sounds being the slurping of their boots as they tramped through the mud and the rustling of the heather. When they reached the crest of a hill, Jonah stopped and pointed into the shadows before them.

"This is where Macleod comes tae meet his friends."

Forrester strained his eyes in an attempt to distinguish anything in the murky blackness. He could hear the sea crashing against the rocks and gradually began to perceive the moonlight glittering on the dark water.

As his eyes adjusted he could pick out the rocky beach where the land met the sea. He followed Jonah a few yards and crouched down beside him at the edge of the cliff.

"Must be careful now," Jonah whispered. "Stay out o' sight."

Forrester buttoned up his coat as far as it would go and blew on his hands in an effort to fend off the biting cold. Jonah uncorked the bottle of whisky they had brought and swigged from it before handing it over.

"Do you think Macleod will come?" Forrester asked.

"He may well." Jonah shrugged. "But he may not. He always meets his friends on those rocks."

Following Jonah's outstretched finger, Forrester stared at the empty black rocks on the other side of the bay. Waves crashed against the towering cliffs and showered the rocks beneath with foam. The wind blew without mercy and Forrester swore under his breath when he began to feel the icy sting of rain against his cheeks.

"Fantastic," he hissed and took a mouthful from the bottle. "What now?"

"Now he gets wet," the hunchback laughed.

***

The rain came down heavily. It poured forth from the grey clouds in sheets and dappled the surface of the churning waters beneath them. Forrester and the hunchback remained seated on the cliff-top, there being little point in trying to find shelter. The rain soaked through their clothes, ran off their shivering skin and pooled around them where they sat.

Forrester gave up wiping the water from his face and allowed it to trickle unimpeded down his brow and along the uneven surface of his nose. His clothes hung heavily and exuded the fusty odour of sodden wool.

A slow uncomfortable hour passed in this manner. Forrester was just about to give up and begin the long trudge back to Stornoway when Jonah reached across and clasped his arm.

"Not yet, Englishman," he hissed, "daes he see the light approach?"

Gazing into the gloom, Forrester eventually spotted the small glimmer of a lantern out at sea. The light drew closer and soon they could see the dark shape of a small row boat reach the shoreline. A shadowy figure leapt from the boat and took hold of the lantern. The light swung from side to side as it was carried over to the rock Jonah had pointed out earlier.

"Is that him?"

"Who else would be out here at this time o' night?"

They watched as the figure holding the lantern made his way to the water's edge. The lantern swung wildly side to side, as if signalling to someone far away. The lantern was swung three times followed by a pause of about half a minute before the swinging recommenced. This pattern was repeated several times and the furtive nature of the signal confirmed Forrester's suspicion that Macleod was up to no good.

From the cliff-top hiding place they watched with bated breath, entranced by the strange spectacle that was being played out beneath them. The signal brought no response from the blank face of the sea though the lantern continued to be swung for much of the next few hours. Forrester and Jonah exchanged no words during this time, an unspoken understanding between them pointed to the need for silence. The figure holding the lantern eventually sat down on a rock but continued to show great patience in his vigil by the water.

The figure was still and his shadowy form blended into the gloom surrounding the rocks. Only the slight movements of the lantern and an occasional cough hinted at any life in the darkness on the other side of the bay.

The hours dragged by and Forrester found himself repeatedly checking his pocket-watch, tutting at the painfully slow progress of the minute hand.

As the darkness began to give way to the encroaching dawn, a grey fog drifted in from the sea. Macleod's deep voice rang out in the bay, echoing from the cliffs and shattering the early morning calm:

Dhèanainn sùgradh ris an nigh`n duibh
'n dèidh dhomh èiridh anns a` mhadainn;
dhèanainn sùgradh ris an nigh`n duibh.

Dhèanainn sùgradh ris a` ghruagaich
nuair a bhiodh an sluagh nan cadal.

Dhèanainn sùgradh an àm dùsgaidh
ri maighdinn ùir nan siùil chairtidh.

Dhèanainn sùgradh ris a' ghruagaich
h-uile uair a bhiodh i agam.

"Is that a song?" Forrester asked under his breath.

"Aye," Jonah answered, "tis a love song from a sailor tae his boat."

Though the fog continued to roll in with the tide, the light was such that it was now possible to see Macleod without too much difficulty. He stood gazing out to sea with his hands clasped behind him and the lantern by his feet. A long barrelled shotgun rested against a nearby rock and beside that was a wooden box containing a number of bottles. Although he was not close enough to see the bottles in any great detail, Forrester would have staked his life that they were the same unlabelled whisky he had sampled on Macleod's boat and in the office of the Chief Magistrate.

Macleod sang with gusto, ignorant of his audience hidden on top of the cliff. Forrester watched the water where Macleod's gaze seemed fixed and suppressed a cry as he saw the strange figure emerge.

The first sign of its presence was a ripple on the water a few dozen yards from the shore. A grey form broke the surface and paddled without a sound to the rocks. Macleod showed no fear as the creature lifted itself from the water and crept over the rocks towards him. If it had stood upright the creature would have towered above Macleod but it held itself hunched over, its long muscular arms reaching towards the ground. Hairless, its grey skin glistened in the pale morning sun. Though slender, the steady, measured way it moved belied a grace and strength that was both terrifying and awe-inspiring.

Macleod waited patiently as the creature approached and was joined by two others that stepped out of the seething waters. The three figures stood motionless before Macleod and listened attentively as he spoke.

Forrester struggled to hear Macleod's words over the noise of the crashing waves. On hands and knees he crawled to the edge of the cliff in the vain hope of catching some of their exchange. A flutter of white wings burst from the cliff-face beneath him as he disturbed a nest of gulls. The four figures turned as one at the sound and Macleod's face contorted in anger when he saw Forrester at the top of the cliff. The creatures shrieked, and plunged back into the sea. A few strokes from their long limbs took them far away from the shoreline. The lead figure gave one final cry before all three vanished beneath the waves.

Macleod reached for his shotgun and pointed it towards the cliff. Forrester needed no more persuasion and rolled out of view as the shotgun roared and peppered the rock face with shot.

Jonah scrambled over to Forrester's side, his eyes wide open with terror. Another blast echoed across the bay and Forrester crawled through the mud with Jonah behind him.

When he was certain they were out of Macleod's line of sight, he stood up and began to hurry back in the direction of town.

They ran for what seemed an age, the rain-soaked ground slowing their progress. Their clothes were not only heavy with water but also caked in the thick black mud of the moor.

Though he glanced over his shoulder frequently and saw no sign of Macleod, Forrester was not convinced that they were out of range of his gun. Jonah followed a short distance behind, wheezing with exertion but offering no complaint.

Forrester's breath burned in his chest and his heart pounded with fright at what he had witnessed. When his legs could take no more he slowed and doubled over, gasping as he tried to control his breathing.

"What the bloody hell were those things?" he asked, when Jonah finally caught up and collapsed by his side.

"Macleod's friends," the hunchback panted. "I told him tae stay out o' sight. He shouldnae hae let them see him."

"Were they human?"

"Human or no'," Jonah wheezed, "they got a good look at him."

Forrester spun about and surveyed the surrounding moor. Aside from a few grazing sheep and the occasional rock pointing up towards the sky, it was empty.

"Where do they come from? Do they live in the sea?"

"Jonah kens little more than he daes. They swims out o' the Minch tae talk wi' Macleod an' then they swims away carryin' a few bottles o' peatreek. Jonah's ne'er seen a man wha' swims as they an' he's ne'er seen a fish wha' walks on land. Jonah's ne'er had the inclination tae walk on down tae the water an' ask 'em what they are."

Forrester did not respond to Jonah's sarcasm and the rest of the walk back to Stornoway passed in sullen silence.

Jonah waved farewell to Forrester at the door of the Royal Hotel. Mindless of his bedraggled and filthy appearance, Forrester stepped into the dining room and took his seat for breakfast. The waitress nearly screamed with surprise when she saw him and, taking him for a vagrant, politely asked him to leave.

"I am a guest at this hotel," he spluttered with indignation. "I haven't slept all night, I've walked through a bloody marsh, been soaked to the skin and shot at. Now, go and fetch me a pot of strong coffee and some bacon and eggs before I start making a scene."

The waitress scurried away and returned quickly with his food. He cleared his plate in a matter of minutes but did not taste the food. The coffee was scalding and though it scorched his tongue as he drank he drained several cups in quick succession. Having breakfasted, he staggered up to his room, kicked off his mud-encrusted clothes and crawled into bed. Overcome with exhaustion, he fell into a deep slumber.

He woke at noon, feeling somewhat refreshed. The events of the previous night seemed distant and unreal, like something from a dream; the long walk across the moor, the endless wait on the cliff-top, the strange creatures from the sea. He sat up and rubbed his face then looked at the pile of filthy clothes lying on the floor. It had been no dream.

He washed and dressed himself, enjoying the sensation of clean clothes against his skin. The mud that covered his greatcoat had dried and he used a clothes brush to make it as presentable as possible. Reaching into its deep pockets, he removed his pistol and spent twenty minutes taking it apart and cleaning it.

The Webley Boxer may well have been over ten years old but Forrester had yet to find a pistol more reliable or one that packed such a punch. Despite the cylinder holding only four bullets, each of the .577 shells was capable of putting a grown man down for good. Once satisfied that the pistol was in good working order, he replaced it in his pocket and left the room.

The midday sun rode high in the clear blue sky. The dark clouds of the previous night had cleared and Forrester was surprised to find himself shivering, despite the brightness. He wandered to North Beach and scanned the faces of the herring girls until he saw Effie Morrison.

Her face broke into a smile when she saw him beckoning and she waved enthusiastically in reply. When the herring girls ceased their work for a short break, she rushed over to the wall where he sat.

"Edmund," she beamed. "This is a surprise... Whatever's the matter?"

"I need to talk to your father again."

"An' there was me thinkin' ye was wantin' tae see me," she pouted.

He placed his hands onto her shoulders and looked into her eyes.

"Effie, you must listen to me. Those things your father told me about, the Blue Men... I think they are real."

"Real?" she laughed. "What're ye talkin' about? The Blue Men are chust a story. They're no more real than dragons or kelpies."

"You don't understand," he grasped her shoulders harder to hide the trembling in his arms. "I saw them."

"Ye... saw them?" she asked incredulously.

"I saw something. Last night. Jonah Macaskill took me out to Arnish moor and... and..."

The words did not come. As he stared at her, he saw the disbelief written on her face. She took one of his hands in hers and rubbed it soothingly.

"Ye're upset. I heard about Colin."

Forrester nodded but said nothing.

"He was a good person," she continued. "It was a terrible accident."

"No." He shook his head. "That was no accident. Macleod was behind it, I'm certain."

"What're ye sayin'?" she gasped.

"We shouldn't talk here." Forrester looked around. "I must speak to your father. I'm going to see him now. Will you meet me there this evening?"

"Tie fingers!" a voice called out.

"That's Boabie," she groaned. "I have tae go."

"Will you meet me at your father's?" he implored.

She gave her assent and hurried back to the farlins. Forrester watched her for a time, wondering whether she believed what he had told her or whether she thought his tale the ramblings of a madman.

***

"English Edmund!" Angus Morrison grinned effusively as he saw Forrester approach.

Forrester grasped the man's hand in greeting and shook it warmly.

"Angus," Forrester offered a weak, apologetic smile, "I'm sorry to disturb you at your work."

"Och, there's nothin' that won't keep till the morrow. Will ye join me for a wee drink?"

Forrester shook his head.

"This isn't a social visit, I'm afraid. You've heard what happened to Colin McCormick?"

"The young cove from Glasgow? Calum's cousin, was he no'? Word travels fast roun' here. Aye, 'tis a nasty business, sure enough."

"I have reason to believe that he was killed by Murdo Macleod and the Blue Men of the Minch."

Though Angus could see that the Englishman spoke in earnest, he struggled to hide his mirth. Forrester related the events of the previous night to the old man. Angus listened carefully as he stared at the distant hills and chewed on his lower lip. When Forrester finished his account, Angus nodded thoughtfully.

"From the mouth o' any other man I'd say that was pure shite, but from a man as straight as yersel' the tale has the ring o' truth."

"On my life I swear it is all true," Forrester said.

"How did ye come tae be mixin' wi' Jonah Crotach? The man's got nae more sense than my coo."

"I'd agree with you if I hadn't seen those... those things." Forrester shuddered at the thought of the creatures.

"Follow me," Angus beckoned and led the way into the thatched blackhouse.

Inside, Forrester was greeted by Caitlin and she forced several cups of sweet tea on him whilst Angus rummaged around in a cupboard and muttered to himself in Gaelic.

"Aha!" he cried triumphantly after a time and emerged holding a long roll of aged brown paper.

Forrester watched as the old man knelt on the floor and carefully unrolled the paper, weighing the edges down with stones.

"A map?" he asked.

"Aye, a gey ol' wan at that. This used tae belong tae my father an' before that it belonged tae his uncle. They were all seanchaidh, like me."

Forrester squinted in the dim light of the blackhouse to see the rough shapes scrawled on the coarse paper. The map represented the islands of the Hebrides from the Long Isle of Lewis and Harris down to Uist and Barra and the countless small islets that speckled Scotland's northwest coast. Spidery scrawls of writing covered almost every available inch of the map in a tongue Forrester was unable to decipher.

"Is that Gaelic?"

"It is."

"You can read it?"

"I can."

"Effie told me you couldn't read."

"Aye, well. There's much Effie disnae ken about this old bodach."

"What does it say?"

"They're stories," Angus smiled, his hard features softening as he gazed at the words, "wee scribblin's o' tales from the islands. This is a map o' stories an' where they are said tae have happened, so we willnae forget what is past."

Angus jabbed a finger at a small collection of islands a short distance from the Long Isle.

"See here. These are the Shiants. The charmed isles."

Forrester looked at the map and felt a shiver go up his spine when he saw the abundance of writing surrounding the islands.

"All this," he pointed at the strange text, "is that all about them?"

"The Blue Men," Angus nodded, "aye. Folks have been talkin' o' them for as long as anyone cares tae remember."

"Is it all true?"

"All stories have a basis in truth, do they no'?" Angus raised his bushy white brows and continued. "The Minch is a dangerous stretch o' water an' the Sound o' Shiant is the worst o' it. D'ye no' think it possible that the stories were told tae keep folks out o' those dangerous currents?"

Forrester rubbed his chin, the growth of stubble scratching his fingers. Angus looked up from the map and met his gaze.

"And what of the Blue Men?" Forrester asked. "How do they fit into these stories?"

"Some say they're angels fallen from heaven. Others believe them tae be the ghosts o' slaves tossed o'erboard. For all I ken they could be the same seals tha' pished sailors mistake for mermaids."

"What I saw was no seal," Forrester grunted.

Angus resumed his study of the map, his finger running beneath the untidy script and his mouth forming soundless words as he read. A few minutes passed in silence before he looked up and cleared his throat.

"There is a tale here that mentions the bay near Arnish

moor. It says tha' two fishermen were pullin' in their nets an' caught up in it was a man, sound asleep an' reekin' o' drink. They haul him intae the boat an' tie him up. He was tall an' thin an' as bald as a haggis. His fingers an' toes was webbed like a frog an' his skin was blue. The men were excited, thinkin' they'd caught somethin' more valuable than fish so they dropped their nets an' started tae row back tae shore. They'd no' gone far when two more Blue Men appears from beneath the waves an' calls out in the Gaelic. The beastie in the boat wakes up an' snaps his bindings as though they was made o' straw then dives intae the waters an' all three o' them vanish."

"This is a true story?" Forrester asked.

"Well, it's written on the map but that disnae make it any more true than one o' those novels folks waste their time readin'."

A sound behind them disturbed their conversation and the men turned to see a figure standing in the doorway. From her slender form, Forrester knew it was Effie but the lack of light in the blackhouse made it impossible to see her face.

"Effie?" Angus asked. "Is that my wee gyurl?"

"It is, father," the figure answered but remained in the shadows.

"Come in an' sit yourself!" Caitlin tore her gaze away from her knitting long enough to call out.

"I saw Macleod, Edmund," Effie said, her voice wavering. "He sends a message tae ye."

"A message?" Forrester asked.

Effie swayed slightly and took a step forward to right herself. As she stumbled into the light, her face was revealed and a collective gasp went around the room. Caitlin cried out and rushed forward, catching her daughter as she sank to the floor. Forrester rose to his feet and watched helplessly as Effie, battered and unconscious, was carried to her parents' bed.

Chapter 9

Caitlin Morrison placed the damp flannel over her daughter's bruised eyes and kissed her gently on the forehead. Her husband sat on the other side of the room in sullen silence, his face occasionally illuminated by the glowing bowl of his pipe.

"Poor wee lamb," Caitlin said. "What kind o' world dae we live in where a man can treat a woman so cruel?"

"He's no man," Angus spat, "he's a beast. An animal. He's the very devil."

"No," Forrester interrupted. "However foul his deeds, Murdo Macleod is just a man. Let's not fool ourselves into thinking he is anything more terrible."

"What can we dae?" Caitlin sobbed.

"Nothin'!" Angus roared. "We'll dae nothin' cause we ken very well what would happen tae us if we were tae bring charges 'gainst the man. We'd find ourselves wi'out a croft, wi'out a roof o'er our heads! Our neighbours wouldnae even stand by us for fear o' gettin' on the wrong side o' the factors!"

"We could leave," Caitlin muttered.

The old man ignored this comment and continued to puff away on his pipe. Caitlin dabbed at the corners of her eyes with a handkerchief and held her daughter's hand. Effie, oblivious to her parents' impotent rage and grief, groaned slightly and continued to sleep.

"Why would he dae such a thing?" Caitlin asked.

"He's sendin' ye a warnin'," Angus glared at Forrester. "Ye've upset him an' he's punishin' us all."

Forrester struck a match and took a few puffs on his cigarette before blowing the flame out.

"Macleod is afraid," he stated. "I saw something I shouldn't have last night and he's worried his secret will get out."

"Whatever it was ye saw, it'd be best for us all if ye forgot it."

Forrester shook his head solemnly.

"I can't do that."

"Look what he's done tae my wee gyurl!" Angus rose to his feet and bellowed. "D'ye no' think ye've done enough harm?"

"This isn't just about Effie. It's about Colin McCormick and Alistair Mackinnon too. Not to mention all the fishermen and crofters who are too scared to stand up to Murdo Macleod. He's hiding something and I intend to find out what it is."

"And how d'ye propose tae dae that?" Caitlin asked, her face pale and her bloodshot eyes swollen from shedding tears.

"I'm going to the Shiants," Forrester answered simply.

"An' how d'ye think ye can get out tae the islands? Ye cannae chust swim there!"

"None of the fishermen from town will take me, that much I know, but I'm sure you know someone with a boat who can take me out there."

"Aye, well, I ken more'n a few lads wi' boats," Angus sighed. "But they'd no' be keen tae be messin' in those waters, Blue Men or no'!"

"Well maybe one of them would loan me the boat and I could find someone to sail it for me."

"Ha!" Angus chortled, his eyes flickering in the firelight. "Ye're certainly keen, Englishman, I'll give ye that! And who, pray tell, would be mad enough tae take a wee trip across the Sound o' Shiant?"

"Jonah Macaskill."

"The Crotach? Ye'd end up in Greenland afore that fool would get ye tae the Shiants."

"Edmund?" Effie's weak voice could barely be heard over the raised voices of the two men. When she spoke again, her mother heard and signalled that they should be quiet in order for her to speak.

"Edmund? It's no' yer fault. It was Macleod an' his men. Ye have tae watch out for them, he said they're goin' tae kill ye. They want Jonah Crotach an' all."

"Where will I find Jonah now?"

"Ye'll often see him drinkin' in town on a night. Chust listen for the sound o' his accordion."

Forrester rose to his feet and headed towards the door.

"Where d'ye think ye're goin'?" Angus asked.

"I'm not about to stand by and let Macleod and his thugs kill again," Forrester snarled. "I'm going to fetch Jonah and when we get back here I'll need you to take me to your friend with the boat."

"But it'll take us all night tae get there!" the old man spluttered.

Forrester did not answer. He took one final look at Effie before he stepped out of the house and into the gathering twilight.

***

Knowing that time was of the essence, he ran most of the way to town. If he dawdled, Macleod and his men might find Jonah before he did. Forrester did not even consider the possibility that he might already be too late to save the hunchback. He focused his mind on his breathing and the steady rhythm of his legs as they pounded down the hill. By the time the lights of Stornoway came into view he was staggering from a cramp in his side and fighting for breath.

His first port of call was the bar of the Royal Hotel. Finding no sign of Jonah there he turned his attention to the numerous other pubs that littered the waterfront. His flushed face and dishevelled appearance turned more than a few heads in the smoky bars. He did not spend long in each of them, his eyes searched the crowds for Jonah and finding nothing, he moved on to the next one. By the time he reached the third pub, the same one in which he had spoken to Effie earlier in the week, Forrester was beginning to worry.

Inside the pub the cacophonous drone of the hunchback's accordion could be heard over the low hum of the inhabitants and Forrester breathed a sigh of relief. He barged through the crowd to the source of the music and grabbed Jonah by the shoulder. Surprised by the interruption, the hunchback stopped playing and turned to face him.

"Och, it's the English," he smiled. "And there was Jonah worryin' Macleod had caught up wi' him."

"Macleod is looking for you. If you come with me now I can protect you from him."

"Oh ho! D'ye hear the English courage?" Jonah laughed aloud. "And who daes he think will protect him from Macleod?"

Forrester was not given the opportunity to answer. Feeling a tap on his shoulder, he turned to see who stood behind him and was thrown backwards as a large fist connected with his jaw. He staggered into the arms of Jonah who continued to laugh at the situation.

"A good job Jonah was here tae help him," he quipped.

The customers of the pub anticipated a brawl and cleared a space around the men by the bar. Macleod stood with his back to the door of the pub. He was accompanied by three large men, one of whom Forrester recognised as Rowan Campbell. Macleod folded his powerful arms across his barrel chest and looked scornfully at Forrester.

"I want ye gone," he growled.

"Don't worry, we're leaving," Forrester answered.

"No' chust the pub," Macleod continued, "I want ye off the islands. Away back tae London or where'er it is ye're from."

Forrester eyes scanned the faces of Macleod and his three thugs.

"I can't do that."

"I'm tellin' ye tae leave."

"You can't do that."

Macleod leaned in closer, his dark eyes narrowing as his brow furrowed.

"Can I no'?"

Forrester straightened up and looked impassively at the burly Scotsman.

"I'm an officer of the law and I'm here to do a job. If you think you can intimidate me in any way then you are sorely mistaken. Now get out of my way and let us past."

One of Macleod's arms stretched out and blocked Forrester's way to the door. Forrester looked down at the faded blue tattoos that covered it and sneered.

"Move your arm before I break it off."

"Those're big words considerin' there's four of us an' chust two of youse."

Forrester's hand disappeared into his pocket and came out gripping the revolver. Macleod's face flushed as he stared down the barrel of the gun. The men behind him shifted uncomfortably and a silence fell on the expectant crowd.

"I still think the odds are in my favour," Forrester said without a hint of amusement.

Macleod's arm dropped and the men moved aside to allow Jonah and Forrester to pass. As they walked out of the pub, Jonah turned to Forrester and looked up at him with a wry smile.

"The Englishman has sand, that's for certain. How can

Jonah return the favour?"

"Follow me," Forrester answered. "We're going on a boat trip."

***

It was nearly ten o'clock by the time Forrester and Jonah returned to the blackhouse on Beinn na Saighde. The night was cold and they huddled by the peat fire, feeling their chills evaporate before its warm glow. The events of the evening had left Forrester feeling exhausted and his eyelids began to grow heavy as he relaxed. He shook off his drowsiness by forcing himself back to his feet and pacing the room.

Effie remained asleep in the bedroom and Caitlin returned from tending to her injuries, shutting the door behind her gently. She looked at Forrester with pity.

"Poor man," she said, "ye're exhausted. Why not get some sleep? The islands will still be there in the morrow."

"No," Forrester answered. "We have to go tonight."

"Will ye have some food tae fill yer stomachs then?"

Jonah's eyes lit up at the mention of food and he licked his lips eagerly. Caitlin handed them some slices of bread and black pudding and they ate in silence, their eyes fixed on the dancing flames of the fire. The door swung open and Angus ducked as he walked under the low door-frame.

"The wagon is ready," he said. "Are we goin'?"

Forrester nodded and helped Jonah to his feet.

"You can leave your accordion here," Forrester said. "I

don't think you'll be needing it where we're going."

They followed Angus out into the cold and clambered onto the hard seat of the wagon. The horse stood in its harness and snorted its disapproval of making a journey at such a strange hour. Angus spoke to it in hushed tones and stroked its neck soothingly. Caitlin hurried out from the blackhouse with a bundle of clothing in her arms.

"Here," she said as she handed Jonah and Forrester each a woollen jumper. "These should keep ye warm tonight. I knitted them myself."

Forrester looked at the jumper in the moonlight and ran his finger along the elaborate ribbed braiding that covered it.

"It's beautiful," he said. "Thank you."

To show their gratitude, both men shrugged off their coats and pulled the jumpers on. Forrester's was a perfect fit though Jonah's hunch meant that his did not suit his twisted form as well. Caitlin smiled at them and wished them luck as Angus cracked the reins and the wagon began its long journey into the darkness.

***

Forrester was used to the comfortable sprung seats of modern carriages so the long journey on the hard wooden bench at the front of Angus Morrison's wagon was not a comfortable one. The road was rough and the old wagon shuddered with every bump. Angus Morrison said nothing for much of the journey, his gaze searching the inky blackness ahead of the horse. Jonah somehow managed to fall asleep in spite of all the discomfort. He rested his head on Forrester's shoulder, his loud snores occasionally punctuated by an unintelligible murmur.

The lights of Stornoway fell away into the distance as the road stretched across the empty moorland. The bare landscape provided little shelter and the wind whipped around them without mercy. Feeling himself begin to shiver, Forrester turned to Angus but the large man seemed unconcerned by the chill. Forrester folded his arms, stuffing his frozen hands into his armpits in the hope that Effie's father would not notice his discomfort.

"It was good of your wife to give us those jumpers," he said, hoping to shatter the frosty silence.

"Mmm," Angus grunted in response.

"She's clearly talented with the knitting needles," he continued. "The patterns on them are fantastic."

"It's a custom that each man on a boat wears a diff'rent knit on their jumpers," Angus said grimly. "Makes it easier tae identify their bodies if they wash up."

A shiver ran up Forrester's spine that had nothing to do with the cold wind. He swallowed drily and wished the old man had kept that piece of information to himself.

A couple of hours later they turned off the main road onto another track. Travelling between a series of small lochs and rocky outcroppings, the track wound endlessly on before them. Their progress was slow. Not only was the track in an even worse condition than the main road, but it snaked and twisted so much that Forrester was unable to determine how far they had gone. The cold wind continued to bite at their exposed skin and Forrester was no longer able to hide his shivers. Jonah stirred from his slumber and yawned as he looked around them.

"Where are we?" he asked.

"The road through Pairc," Angus answered. "I've a friend wi' an ol' skiff in Lemreway."

"A skiff?" Jonah sniffed. "Daes he no' have a bigger boat?"

"What's wrong with a skiff?" Forrester asked.

"Nothin'," Jonah smiled. "Nothin's wrong wi' a skiff if ye're chust paddlin' round a loch. They dinnae fare so well in the open sea."

"It'll have tae," Angus retorted. "Jimmy hasnae got another and I cannae think o' any other man who'd lend ye a boat."

Jonah muttered something under his breath and closed his eyes. Within a few minutes he was sleeping again, his snores mocking Forrester's own weariness. Forrester tried to find a position on the bench that he found comfortable but however he shifted his weight, he still managed to feel every jolt of the wagon at the base of his spine.

"Ye could try layin' on some o' those sacks in the back." Angus pointed a thumb over his shoulder. "It'll be a few more hours afore we get tae the village an' ye've got a long day ahead o' ye."

Forrester thanked Angus and clambered onto the back of the wagon. A pile of empty hessian sacks were heaped in one corner and Forrester found that after arranging them they made a serviceable - if somewhat scratchy - bed. Though he did sleep, the unremitting bumping of the wagon meant that his slumber was not as deep as he had hoped. It did, however, pass a few hours and when he next opened his eyes he saw the clouds behind them tinged with red to herald the emerging sun. Forrester looked at his pocket-watch. It was just before seven o'clock.

"How are we doing, Angus?" Forrester yawned.

Angus turned in his seat and looked bleary-eyed at Forrester.

"We'll be there shortly," he said, "but we can still turn back. An' I willnae think the less o' ye."

The wagon crawled up a steep incline and when they reached the top, Forrester caught his first glimpse of Lemreway. The small village comprised of a few blackhouses that dotted the rocky terrain down to the shore. Past the village, Forrester could see the gently undulating sea and a few empty boats rising and falling on the ebb tide. A short distance from the shore was a green island. There was a peak on either side of the island, both of which were inhabited by a number of grazing sheep. In between the two peaks was a low-lying area where a group of small cottages nestled close together.

"That's not one of the Shiants is it?" Forrester asked.

"No," Angus shook his head. "That's Eilean Liubhaird. The Shiants are much further out. Four families live on Liubhaird. It makes the Shiants look like Edinburgh."

Forrester scanned the horizon for the other islands but saw nothing.

"I can't see them. How far out are they?"

"Five or six miles," Angus answered. "There's a deal o' fog today but ye can see them on a clear day."

Their conversation awoke Jonah. The hunchback stretched himself and looked at the grey horizon. He shook his head and sighed disconsolately.

"He shouldnae be sailin' in this weather."

"We have no choice."

"There's always choice," Jonah frowned. "It's the one thing a man always has."

The wagon descended the hill into the village and came to a stop near a blackhouse in desperate need of repair. The dry-stone walls were crumbling in places and the thatch covering the roof showed signs of decay. Angus climbed down from his seat and entered the house without knocking. Moments later he emerged accompanied by a wiry old man whose tattered clothes hung on his emaciated frame.

"This is Jimmy Munro," Angus said.

Hearing his name, the old man smiled toothlessly and raised a hand in greeting.

"I suppose Angus has told you why we're here?" Forrester said.

"Dè thuirt thu?" Munro said.

"No sense ye talkin' tae him in English," Angus said, "he only speaks the Gaelic."

Angus turned to Munro and chattered away to him in the alien tongue. Forrester listened carefully but could barely distinguish one word from the other, let alone understand what the conversation was about. Seeing his confusion, Jonah leaned over and cupped a hand to Forrester's ear.

"Dinnae worry," he whispered. "He's askin' about the boat, sure enough."

Jimmy Munro did not seem happy with the idea of his boat being taken by an Englishman and the hunchback. He shook his head repeatedly and pointed to the horizon. Angus Morrison was not easily deterred and repeated the offer several times before the old man finally relented.

"He's agreed." Angus clapped his hands and beamed. "Ye

can have his boat for a day but ye must promise tae look after it. If ye lose the boat, Jimmy loses his livelihood, y'ken?"

"We'll take good care of it," Forrester promised. "I'll pay for any damage."

"See that ye do." Angus ran a hand through his beard. "And take care o' yerselves. If what ye say is true, there's worse things out there than foul weather."

Chapter 10

The first sight of the boat did not inspire confidence. The skiff rested in the shallows a short distance from Lemreway's beach. The pale morning light glinted on the water and the faded paintwork of the hull. A short mast rose from the centre of the boat on which hung a tatty canvas sail. Forrester felt a sinking feeling in his stomach as they approached and he saw that the boat was little over eight feet long, substantially smaller than the Manannán.

"Is it safe to go out to sea in this?" he asked Jonah.

Jimmy Munro gave a gummy smile and signalled that they should follow him onto the beach. Standing on the pebbles, they watched the old man wade out into the water and grab hold of the rope that was fixed to its bow.

"Small wonder he's lettin' us take it," Jonah muttered. "If Jonah owned such a wreck he'd be givin' it away. The bodach is probably hopin' tae lose it."

Munro hauled on the line and the underside of the boat scraped on the rocks beneath. He beckoned to the men and they approached warily. Munro held the boat steady as they clambered in and gave it a shove to push it into the deeper water. Jonah wrenched a pair of oars from under the thwarts and fixed them into the rusting rowlocks. One of the oars was shorter than the other and this initially caused Jonah some difficulties. Once he established a more comfortable rhythm, he managed to paddle the boat in a straight line and they headed away from the shoreline.

He rowed in silence, occasionally glancing over his shoulder to check they were a safe distance from the rocks around Eilean Liubhaird. Forrester sat watching Lemreway grow smaller in the distance and eventually disappearing behind the bulk of the island that sheltered the natural harbour.

Once satisfied that he had rowed far enough, Jonah hauled the oars back in and set to raising the sail. Like the rest of the boat, the sail showed signs of age. It had been torn in several different places and crude stitching held the patches in place. The lines attached to the tattered canvas were so frayed that Forrester was surprised not to see them break when the sail caught the wind and billowed outwards. The skiff lurched forward and Jonah whooped with glee as the boom swung over their heads.

"Steady on!" Forrester cried out.

"Calm down," the hunchback winked. "Jonah's chust gettin' a feel for her. It's been more'n a few years since he was last in a boat!"

"How many years?" Forrester asked, feeling his stomach sink a little further.

"He's no cause tae worry. Jonah's an islander. A Lewisman who cannae handle a boat is like fish that cannae swim."

Sure to his word, Jonah proved surprisingly adept at

handling the small craft and they skimmed across the water at an exhilarating speed. The sun was climbing higher in the sky and its warmth was a welcome relief after the cold night. Forrester closed his eyes and breathed in the clean, salty air. He plunged one of his hands into the cool, clear water and smiled as he felt the current buffet his skin.

"That's the first time Jonah's seen the Englishman smile."

"It really is most relaxing out here," Forrester replied.

"Relaxin'?" Jonah scoffed. "Here he is, sailin' intae the Sound o' Shiant, an' he says he's relaxin'! And they say Jonah's mad."

An hour later the coastline of Lewis had slipped away and was little more than a dark shape behind them. Ahead of them stretched a vast expanse of sea and Forrester began to feel more and more vulnerable. He watched Jonah work the rudder with one hand, the other clutching the frayed end of rope attached to the mast and could not help but admire the ease at which the hunchback was able to manoeuvre the small boat.

And that was the problem. The boat was very small and the sea around them was very, very large indeed. Swallowing his nerves, Forrester fixed his eyes ahead of him and searched the horizon for the Shiants. The early morning fog had lifted to the extent that there was only a slight haze but there was still no sign of the islands.

"Which direction would they be in?" Forrester asked.

Jonah looked at the sun and muttered to himself for a moment before he pointed over one side of the boat.

"They'll be lyin' that ways," he answered. "Can he no' see them yet?"

"No," Forrester gazed discontentedly in the direction Jonah

had indicated. "I can't see a bloody th-"

No sooner had the words left his mouth did he spot them. Rising out of the sea were the three black shapes he had seen from the Manannán. The longer he stared the clearer they became and Forrester was soon able to pick out the waves crashing against the towering cliffs and the rich green pasture that covered them.

Jonah hauled on the rope and allowed the boom to swing across. The sail caught the wind and drove the ship onwards, straight towards the largest island.

"We must be quick gettin' tae shore," Jonah said. "These waters are all Macleod's an' he's already not best pleased wi' Jonah."

"I see no other boats," Forrester said, glancing around them.

"Let's no' forget that Macleod's friends are rather fond o' the water," Jonah answered.

Hearing these words, Forrester found his gaze drawn to the sea. The bright sun played on the surface but the fathomless depths beneath them were shrouded in gloom. Down there, somewhere, lurked the strange creatures he had glimpsed that night at Arnish Moor.

"Is this the fastest we can go?" he asked, suppressing a shudder.

The small boat drew closer to the islands and Forrester looked with interest at the land that lay before them. Jutting out of the sea stood the largest of the islands, which Jonah informed him was known as Garbh Eilean, the rough island. Its huge cliffs of basalt towered above the sea, imposing themselves upon the landscape like some monstrous citadel.

The cliffs were formed of rock columns that, although natural, appeared to have been carved by man.

"It's a different rock tae that o' the Long Isle," Jonah commented, seeing Forrester's awe as he gazed at the strange formations.

Approaching from the north, Jonah manoeuvred the boat into the bay which lay between the three islands. To the east lay the smallest island, Eilean Mhuire. On its grassy banks a handful of sheep sat huddled against the wind that swept across its high cliffs. Joined to Garbh Eilean by a tidal causeway was the more hospitable-looking Eilean an Tigh, house island. The boat stayed close to its cliffs as they skirted the southernmost point of the island and headed up the western side.

"Are we not taking a rather long route?" Forrester asked. "Surely it would have been quicker following the west coast of the rough island straight down?

"Aye, that'd be quicker sure enough," Jonah grimaced. "But there's a family o' rocks they call Galtachean that we'd have tae pass on that side. One strong wind would push us ontae them an' we'd be finished."

Following Jonah's outstretched arm Forrester saw the line of large black rocks that thrust out from the churning depths. He shuddered as he imagined what it would be like for the skiff to be smashed to firewood against them.

Forrester breathed a sigh of relief when the boat approached the causeway between Garbh Eilean and Eilean an Tigh. Whilst he had initially enjoyed the journey by boat, the endless miles of empty sea had taken their toll and he looked forward to feeling solid ground beneath his feet once more. Once the sail was lowered Jonah used the oars to pull the boat to the beach of scree that lay between the islands.

The small stones on the beach crunched beneath the bow of the boat and the men clambered out into the shallow surf to haul the vessel past the line of seaweed that marked the highest point of the tide. Further up the beach a series of crude steps were carved into the solid rock of the cliff. Forrester sat on the bottom step and smoked a cigarette whilst Jonah fastened the mooring line to a large metal hoop driven into a rock.

"And what daes the English have planned, eh?" Jonah asked as he approached.

"I want to talk to the family who live here," Forrester said. "We'll need to find them."

"Jonah thinks one of 'em has found him," the hunchback said, staring over Forrester's shoulder.

A shadow fell across the steps and Forrester turned to see the cause of it. The man who stood above him was huge. He was close to seven feet tall and was almost as broad as two men standing shoulder to shoulder. There was not an inch of fat on him and he had the muscular physique of one who had spent many hours labouring in the fields. Despite his intimidating size, the man's face seemed strangely innocent, devoid of any malice or guile.

Forrester pushed himself to his feet and extended his hand in greeting.

"Good day, sir," he smiled.

The huge man clasped his hand in a bone-crushing grip and stared at him, his mouth hanging open. Not wanting to appear rude, Forrester endured the pain and shook the great paw as enthusiastically as he felt able. The man said nothing but remained gazing blankly at him.

"Perhaps he doesn't understand English," Forrester said.

"Say hello to him in Gaelic."

"Madainn mhath," Jonah said.

The giant did not acknowledge Jonah's greeting, nor did he release his grip and the painful handshake continued.

"A bheil Gàidhlig agaibh?" Jonah asked, raising his voice a little louder.

The words did not appear to reach the giant who stared vacantly at Forrester whilst still shaking his hand with relentless enthusiasm. Eventually, Forrester managed to free himself and took a step back from the huge man, massaging his mangled digits.

"Do you understand us?" he yelled.

The giant's face remained impassive. His huge arms hung limply by his sides and his watery eyes moved from one man to the other. His head was covered with closely cropped blonde hair. Despite being cut short, it still appeared dirty and unkempt, much like the threadbare jacket he wore over a collarless shirt. His trousers had clearly been designed for a shorter man and terminated some way above his ankles. The giant's enormous feet were bare and so filthy that Forrester doubted they had ever been washed.

"He's deaf an' dumb," Jonah muttered. "We'd get more sense out o' the rocks."

"Who is he?"

"He must be Big Donald's eldest. Folks call him the balabhan."

The giant turned and began to climb the rough steps cut into the cliff. Forrester and Jonah exchanged a puzzled glance to one another then followed. The steps were steep but the giant was able to take two or three at a time. Jonah and Forrester lagged behind, surprised by the speed at which their silent guide was able to move. He did not pause at the top of the cliff to check that they were following but strode onwards.

In the distance Forrester could see a small house. It was a modern construction, its whitewashed walls standing out against the lush green meadows that surrounded it. A thin plume of smoke escaped from its chimney and drifted into the skies. The giant ambled towards it, his great hands stuffed into his pockets, seemingly unconcerned whether his new companions followed him or not.

The door to the cottage was thrown open and a woman wearing a brown headscarf stepped out. She raised a hand in greeting when she saw the giant approach and watched with interest as he drew closer, the two men following a short distance behind. The woman shielded her eyes from the sun in order to get a better look at the strangers. Though stout, she was by no means plump and wore simple but functional attire. Her small eyes cast suspicious glances at both of them and her thin lips pursed as though tasting something bitter. Forrester guessed that she was in her early fifties and realised immediately that she had taken a dislike to them.

"Dè tha thu ag iarraidh?" she asked accusingly.

Jonah stepped forward and nodded his head in acknowledgement of her before speaking in such rapid Gaelic that Forrester doubted even the woman would be able to understand. She nodded solemnly in response and answered with a few curt words.

"She's Catherine Campbell," Jonah explained. "Big Donald's wife. She's surprised tae see us here. They dinnae get many visitors."

"Does she speak English?" Forrester asked.

"That's no' likely," Jonah shook his head. "The woman can barely speak a civil word in the Gaelic."

Catherine Campbell placed her hands on her hips and glared at them. Forrester smiled awkwardly, hoping he could somehow melt her icy demeanour.

"Where is this Big Donald then?" he asked Jonah.

Jonah translated the question into Gaelic and received a succinct response from the woman.

"He's no' here," Jonah explained. "He's tendin' the sheep."

"Are ye chust goin' tae stand there or will ye come in and have a cup o' tea?" a female voice called out.

The voice came from a pretty face that leaned out of an open window. She was young, no older than seventeen or eighteen and had fair hair that possessed a natural curliness. The girl disappeared from the window and reappeared by her mother's side.

"We've been watchin' the boat come round the islands for the past hour," she chirped. "We were wonderin' if ye were lost."

"We're not lost, miss," Forrester replied, thankful that at least one member of the family was able to speak English. "We've come to speak to your father."

"Father?" The girl frowned. "We're no' behind on the rent again, are we?"

"Nothing of the sort. We need to ask him some questions."

"Well, come in then," she threw her head back and smiled, setting her curls dancing. "Dinnae worry yourselves about mother. She's suspicious of any men who come a-callin'."

Jonah and Forrester followed the family inside the cottage and took a seat around the large table in the kitchen. Forrester surreptitiously watched the young lady as she moved gracefully around the kitchen, aware that the mother sat on the other side of the room and kept a watchful eye on the visitors.

The girl introduced herself as Catriona Campbell, the youngest daughter of the family. She threw her arms about the great neck of the giant and giggled as her legs were lifted off the floor.

"This is my brother, John," she shrieked as he swung her around.

They were soon joined by another sibling. As Mor Campbell stepped into the room, Forrester immediately understood why the mother watched her visitors so carefully. Like her younger sister, Mor was strikingly beautiful. Unlike her sister, her hair was dark and her skin was dusky as though she had a trace of Spanish blood in her. She was also heavily pregnant and Forrester noticed that she did not wear a wedding ring. She eased herself into a chair with a sigh and fluttered her eyelids at the guests.

"What brings ye tae the Shiants?" Mor asked.

"They're here tae see father," Catriona answered before Forrester had a chance to speak.

"I can't think o' the last time we had visitors," Mor said, smiling coquettishly.

"I can," Catriona smirked. "It would be about eight months past."

Mor threw her sister an angry look and turned back to Forrester.

"Ye're English," she said, toying with a lock of her hair.

"That's right," Forrester answered.

"Have ye seen Edinburgh?" Catriona asked eagerly. "I long tae see a big city."

"Edinburgh is in Scotland, ye ninny," Mor scolded.

"I was chust askin'," the younger girl sulked.

"I've never seen Edinburgh," Forrester answered, "but I hear it is beautiful."

"The biggest town I've ever been tae is Stornoway," Catriona grumbled. "We went over two years past an' I'm still wearin' the same dress we bought there."

Mor rolled her eyes as her younger sister bewailed her lack of clothes. She had clearly heard the same complaints many times before. Her eyes moved from Forrester and settled on Jonah. More specifically, they settled on Jonah's back which she stared at with distaste.

"What's wrong wi' your back?" she asked.

"Jonah's back is his own business," he answered indignantly. "Why does she no' ask the Englishman what's wrong wi' his nose, or ask herself what's wrong wi' her stomach?"

Mor's cheeks coloured and her hands circled her bump protectively.

"My sister's expectin' a bairn," Catriona sneered. "Ye should've heard the uproar when she broke the news tae father, they'd have heard him yellin' on the mainland."

"Will your father be back soon?" Forrester asked, hoping to ease the growing tension between the two young women.

"Father was out tendin' the sheep on Garbh Eilean," Mor answered. "He'll have seen ye land on the beach and will be headin' over here, no doubt."

Catriona poured everyone in the room a cup of tea and prepared slices of bread and butter. Forrester ate in silence, listening to the sisters throw thinly disguised insults at one another. Jonah crammed the slices of bread into his mouth as though afraid he would never eat again. When he saw Catherine Campbell staring at him, he winked at her and slurped his tea. The old woman shook her head and began jabbering at him in Gaelic.

"She says ye've the table manners of a pig," Mor helpfully translated. "She says ye should learn some manners."

"Jonah can understand the Gaelic perfectly well," Jonah scowled. "Old mother's manners tae strangers are none that fine neither."

"Feashar math?" a deep voice boomed from outside, providing a merciful distraction from the mounting hostility in the kitchen.

The door swung open and a huge man filled the empty frame. He was as tall and as powerfully built as the balabhan but noticeably older. A sparse covering of grey hair topped a face whose weathered skin appeared to have the texture of wrinkled leather. The older giant pulled off a pair of enormous boots and removed his jacket before he approached the table. He picked up one of the delicate china teacups and drained its contents in one gulp before grinning broadly at the two visitors.

"Dè an t-ainm a tha oirbh?" he asked.

Mor exchanged a few words in Gaelic to her father who nodded slowly as he lowered himself into one of the chairs. He studied Forrester and Jonah with interest. Some men will glance at the face of another and then look away as though ashamed. Big Donald Campbell was not such a man. His eyes lingered on them as though reading something in their features. Forrester's hand subconsciously moved to his flattened nose and massaged the mangled cartilage. Jonah was less intimidated by the large man's stare, being well accustomed to the inquisitive gazes of perfect strangers.

Minutes passed in awkward silence before Campbell barked an order to his wife in Gaelic. The old woman hurried over to the sideboard and returned bearing three glasses and a dusty bottle of whisky. Campbell opened the bottle and filled the glasses without ceremony. It did not escape Forrester's notice that the glasses were of a superior quality to the sort one would expect to find in the house of a crofter. They were weighty and were decorated with an etching of a thistle. These were not glasses for everyday usage but the sort reserved for special occasions. Campbell pushed a glass to each of the men and raised the one before him.

"Slàinte mhòr agad!" he smiled.

Chapter 11

With a wave of an enormous hand, Campbell dismissed the women from the room. His wooden chair creaked as he leaned back to swallow the remaining drops of whisky from his glass. Following his lead, Jonah placed his empty glass on the table and smacked his lips with pleasure. Campbell moved to refill the empty glasses but raised his eyebrows when he saw that Forrester's glass remained untouched.

"He should drink up," Jonah warned. "It's impolite no' tae keep pace wi' the host."

"I'm sick of drinking bloody whisky," Forrester muttered. "Does everything in Scotland have to start with a drink? Tell him I need to ask some questions."

Though Campbell could not understand Forrester's words, he could clearly understand the meaning of the untouched glass. He turned to his son who stood in the corner like some vast monolith and called him over. John lumbered over to the table, took Forrester's whisky and drained it with one gulp.

Campbell spoke in Gaelic to Jonah who nodded and smiled

before translating.

"Donald says that if ye're no' drinkin' wi' us, the boy can have your share."

"Very well," Forrester replied as the glasses were refilled. "Ask him about the Blue Men."

Jonah fired a rapid series of questions at Campbell but the man simply answered each one with a shake of his head and a blunt word or two. A few minutes passed this way before Jonah threw up his hands and gave an exasperated cry.

"The man'll no' tell us a thing."

"He doesn't know about them?"

"Ach, he kens them, that much is clear," Jonah cried. "He says he cannae talk about them. He's sore afeared o' speakin' openly."

"Is it Macleod?" Forrester asked. "Tell him that himself and his family are safe from Murdo Macleod whilst I'm here."

Jonah translated and Campbell slapped his hand on the table and bawled with laughter. Forrester did not have to speak Gaelic to understand that the man had no fear of Macleod.

"Big Donald says that he'd sooner be afeared o' a Guga than a bollsgaire such as Murdo Macleod," Jonah said. "He says that Macleod an' his ruffians daren't come tae the islands for fear o' what dwells beneath."

"What does he mean? What dwells beneath?"

"The man willnae say," Jonah groaned. "Jonah keeps askin' him that but he daren't say more."

"Offer him money" Forrester said, scattering a handful of coins on the table.

Campbell shook his head again and leaned back in his chair. He spat a few terse words at Jonah and folded his arms decisively across his chest.

"Big Donald disnae want your money," Jonah explained. "He says he'd rather be alive an' poor than rich an' drowned."

Forrester scooped the money back into his hand and rose from his seat. He walked to small window that looked out to sea and sighed.

"Would Mister Campbell have any objection to us having a look around the island?" he asked.

Having translated the question, Jonah listened to Campbell's answer before he joined Forrester at the window.

"Big Donald says we're no' tae wander the island an' disturb his sheep," Jonah said, adding in a whisper, "Has the English ever heard such shite?"

"He's hiding something," Forrester agreed.

"He wants us tae stay the night here," Jonah continued. "Then we're tae get off the island at first tide. He disnae want strange men around his daughters."

"Tell him we're grateful to have a roof over our heads for the night," Forrester instructed, not taking his eyes off the expanse of water in the distance, "and tell him to rest easy, we won't be interfering with his flock or his daughters."

***

Jonah lay slumped across the table with his head resting on his hands. Their attempts to extract any more information from

Donald Campbell had proved wholly unsuccessful and Jonah had drowned his disappointment with the remainder of the whisky.

Forrester had politely declined taking a drink and had watched the hunchback drink himself into a stupor before mumbling something about a sore head and slipping into unconsciousness. Catherine and Mor bustled into the room carrying blankets shortly after Campbell and his son had excused themselves and retired to their beds. Forrester arranged his blankets in front of the fireplace and made a great show of making himself comfortable whilst Mor draped a blanket over Jonah's disfigured shoulders. As soon as the women had left the room, Forrester leapt to his feet and shook Jonah until he awoke.

"Wh- what the bloody hell?" he murmured, sitting up groggily and surveying the room with bleary eyes. "What daes he think he's doin'? Jonah's steamin' drunk and chust wants tae sleep."

"Do you think we came all this way just for you to get arseholed and sleep in a shepherd's kitchen?" Forrester hissed. "We're going out to take a look around."

Jonah grumbled as he staggered to his feet and followed Forrester to the door. Having lifted a small lantern from where it hung on the wall, Forrester was able to open the door with little more than a slight creak of the hinges. The two men stepped out into the night and shut the door behind them. They hurried away from the cottage, running a hundred yards across the grass before slowing their pace and checking that nobody had seen their exit. The lantern cast a circle of light about them and in its pale glow Forrester could see that Jonah was feeling the ill effects of the whisky.

"There was Jonah havin' the nicest dream," the hunchback

wailed, "warm sun and golden sand. Then the English shakes him awake an' drags him aways tae stumble about in the dark. This is no' fun."

"I never said it would be fun," Forrester retorted.

"Aye, but he ne'er said it'd be this shite neither."

Jonah continued to complain as they made their way along the cliff-top. Hidden by the darkness, they could hear the waves pounding against the rocks beneath them. Occasionally, Forrester would pause and stare into the shadows at the foot of the cliffs, his eyes searching for any sign of life. Seeing nothing, he would shake his head and they would resume their weary trudging.

"What daes he think he'll see?" Jonah griped. "The rocks're black, the waters black... He's chasin' shadows in the dark."

They walked on, always keeping the cliff on their right hand side. Forrester would have liked to have moved quicker but the alcohol had left Jonah unsteady on his feet. On several occasions he stumbled into Forrester or toppled over and lay on his back giggling at the night sky. After walking in silence for some time, he began to sing, quietly at first but gradually building in both confidence and volume.

As I was walkin' all alone,
I heard twa corbies makin' a moan,
The one tae the other daes say,
Where shall we gang an' dine this day?

In behind yon old fell dyke
I ken there lies a new slain knight
And naebody kens that he lies there

But his hawk, his hound, his lady fair.

His hound is tae the huntin' gone,
His hawk tae fetch the wild-fowl home,
His lady's ta'en another mate,
So we shall make our dinner sweet.

"A charming song," Forrester commented under his breath. "Do you have anything more cheerful?"

"Daes the night deserve better?"

Forrester was about to respond when his eyes caught a slight movement on the shore. He pushed Jonah to the ground and dived down next to him. Having covered the lantern with Forrester's greatcoat, they crawled to the edge of the cliff and gazed down the precipitous drop to the rocks that lay beneath.

On a large, flat outcropping above the waves lay a dark form. Forrester signalled for silence and gazed at the shape, wondering if what he had seen a moment before was merely a trick of the light. He knew that it was not his imagination when he heard Jonah draw a sharp breath. They watched with growing horror as the shape gave a short jerky movement as though dragging itself further onto the rock before lying still once more.

"Is... is that one of those things?" he whispered.

"Who can tell?" Jonah replied. "There's somethin' there but Jonah cannae tell him what it is."

"Whatever it is, it's as big as a man."

"Look!" Jonah grabbed Forrester's arm. "There's another!"

The men held their breath as they watched a second form emerge from the water and slither onto the rock beside the first.

Forrester edged back to his greatcoat and removed the revolver from within its pocket. He felt a surge of confidence as he crawled back to Jonah's side, gripping the weapon. Without a word he straightened his arm and took aim along the Webley's short barrel.

"Is he goin' tae kill it?" Jonah asked.

Forrester did not answer the question but gently squeezed the trigger, watching the hammer lift ever so slightly. The shadowy figures on the rocks shifted their positions and Forrester altered his aim so that he drew a bead on the larger of the two. His heartbeat racing, he watched his arm rise and fall with each breath he drew. He exhaled as he tightened his finger on the trigger and watched the hammer begin to move once more.

"Are ye sure ye want tae be playin' wi' that?"

The voice startled the men. They had been so absorbed with the creatures on the rocks at the foot of the cliff that they had neglected to keep watch for anything nearby. Jonah allowed a cry of terror to escape his lips before he clamped a hand over his mouth. Forrester reacted as one who is accustomed to skirmishing, rolling over on his back and pointing the pistol at the figure that had crept up behind them.

"Come now Mister Forrester," Mor Campbell chuckled. "I'm sure ye can think o' better things tae do wi' your weapon than point it at innocent young gyurls. Or the seals, for that matter."

Forrester felt the blood rush to his cheeks and was thankful that the darkness would go some way to hiding his embarrassment.

"Seals?" he spluttered, looking at the indistinct shapes lying on the rock beneath them. "Is that what they are?"

"Of course they are, ye daftie," she laughed, her hands curled around her pregnant belly protectively. "What did ye think they were?"

"Did ye follow us?" Jonah asked.

"Och, it wasnae hard," she replied. "I dinnae sleep well at the moment, what with havin' tae piss six times a night an' I heard ye creepin' out. I wondered what ye were up tae an' decided tae follow. That lantern and the sound o' yer singin' didn't exactly make it difficult followin'."

Forrester threw an angry look at Jonah before turning back to face Mor.

"Does anyone else know we're here?"

"I doubt it. The only thing that'll wake mother an' father once they're asleep is the cock crowin' at dawn. Catriona was fast asleep when I left her."

"And your brother?"

"Och, ye dinnae have tae worry about him. Even if he was awake he'd no' be able tae tell a soul about it and wouldnae have the sense tae follow us. Your wee secret is safe with me."

Forrester breathed a sigh of relief and stuffed the revolver back into his pocket. Mor watched him out of the corner of her eye as she steadily lowered herself onto a patch of soft heather.

"D'ye always travel wi' a gun?" she asked.

"I've always found it better to have one and not need it than to need one and not have it."

"What were ye askin' father?"

"I'm looking for something."

"Somethin' or someone?" she asked, raising her eyebrows

expectantly.

"Some things, to be precise," he answered. "Your father wasn't too forthcoming with his answers."

"He's no' the most talkative man," she gently stroked her swollen middle as she spoke. "Him and mother have no' been best welcomin' tae strangers since I had my wee accident."

"What do you know about the Blue Men?" Forrester asked.

"Ye shouldnae be askin' about those," she shuddered.

"Why not?"

"It's nae more than a tale told by old coves tae frighten wee bairns," Mor said, her eyes avoiding Forrester's and focusing on the murky waves breaking at the foot of the cliffs.

"She's a fine gyurl," Jonah crowed, "but she's a terrible liar."

"I couldn't agree with you more," Forrester said. "Come now, Mor. What can you tell us about the Blue Men?"

Mor shook her head and pursed her lips. She plucked anxiously at the patch of heather on which she sat.

"Father told me no' tae talk about them," she sniffed.

"Your father isn't here," Forrester spoke soothingly, "and I can assure you that whatever you tell us will remain a secret between the three of us."

"Is that a promise?"

"The Englishman disnae lie," Jonah said, staggering to his feet and stretching. "He's one o' the few she can trust."

Mor looked from Forrester to Jonah and then back again. Her eyes searched his features, as if looking for some mark of dishonesty.

"Very well," she said, "I'll show ye what ye want tae see."

She turned and began to walk away from them, keeping the cliff face on her right hand side. Jonah stuck out a grubby hand to help Forrester to his feet and they followed without a word. They did not have to walk far before she stopped and peered down the near-vertical cliff face.

"This is Leòidean Mòra," Mor stated and extended an arm to point into the darkness, "out there is Eilean Mhuire. Ye'll find what ye're lookin' for there."

Forrester peered into the darkness and could just distinguish the dark shape of the eastern island of the Shiants. He stroked his moustache as he considered the distance.

"We'll take the boat and go out there at first light," he said resolutely. "With any luck your father will assume we've headed back to Stornoway. Do you think you could keep his attention away from that island for the day?"

Mor grabbed Jonah roughly and spoke to him in Gaelic. Though he could not understand the words, Forrester could detect the pleading, impassioned tone of her voice. Jonah nodded and answered her curtly before he cleared his throat and spat onto the grass.

"What does she say? Why won't she talk in English?"

"Peace, man," Jonah heaved a sigh and ran a hand through his hair. "The gyurl is pure scared."

"Scared? Scared of what?"

"She says that on Eilean Mhuire is a ruined chapel. Chust tae the west o' the ruins we'll find the steepest cliffs. There's an openin' intae the caves on that cliff face that ye can see at low tide. Inside those caves dwell unspeakable things."

Seeing Mor begin to shake, Forrester stepped close to her and spoke quietly, hoping to soothe her nerves.

"Those things you talk of," he said, "we've seen them before. I have reason to believe they are responsible for the death of a young lad from Lewis and a friend of mine. If they're dangerous, your whole family could be at risk here."

"No," she trembled, "they willnae harm us. Father has an agreement with 'em. He disnae interfere in their business an' they leave us be. But if ye disturb 'em, who can say what they'll dae?"

"How long has your father had this arrangement?"

"Mother an' father have been here near twenty years. They moved here wi' John after the death o' the twins. For the early years they didnae think there was anythin' livin' on the islands but the sheep an' the birds. The year I was born they lost a few sheep every month but father always reckoned they'd been swept away by the waves. The first attacks started chust after Catriona was born. I still have nightmares about those horrible nights. We'd gather by the hearth an' listen tae them prowlin' outside an' scratchin' at the door. Mother would sing tae try an' hide the sounds o' those things screechin' an' hollerin'. Father would chust sit there wi' the gun pointed at the door in case one broke through. Catriona was chust a bairn an' didnae understand. She must've thought it was a game an' she'd laugh each time the door shook."

Mor pulled her shawl about her shoulders and shivered. Forrester offered her his greatcoat but she declined with a shake of her head.

"Why did your family stay?" he asked.

"We had tae stay. Father was employed by Paddy Sellar tae tend the islands. We couldnae go anywhere else."

"Why did the attacks on the house stop?"

"One day, Father an' John found one o' them at the foot o' the cliffs. It must've found a cask o' whisky washed up 'cause it was dead-drunk an' couldnae even crawl back tae water, let alone stand. Father was fixin' tae kill it but it looked at him an' he saw somethin' in its eyes that made him stay his hand. Him an' John rowed it back out tae Eilean Mhuire. Chust before it flopped intae the water it turned tae father an' spoke tae him."

"It spoke to him?" Forrester gasped.

"Aye, in the Gaelic. But father says it was strange, old-fashioned like... like the Gaelic spoken by the old coves. It said it was Gille Meic Uilleim an' that it would remember his kindness so long as we kept away from the caves."

"And they've left you alone since then?"

"Not a sign o' them. Can ye see why father disnae want tae talk o' it? Will ye reconsider goin' out there?"

"The blone might as well be askin' the tide tae flow backwards," Jonah scoffed.

Forrester did not answer Mor's question, his unwavering gaze fixed on the dark waters that churned between the two islands.

Chapter 12

Forrester struck a match and cupped the small flame in his hand. Shielded from the wind, he lit two cigarettes before handing one to Jonah. The two men sat in silence and smoked as the first glimmer of dawn began to emerge from behind Eilean Mhuire. The sea was calm and there were few clouds in the sky.

"A good wind," Jonah commented. "It should get us across tae the caves afore Big Donald is even risen from his bed."

"I certainly hope so," Forrester replied, his eyes fixed the distant cliffs of the island as the morning light crept across their rugged surface.

Mor Campbell had sat with the men for a little over an hour before her patience ran thin and she crept back to the house alone. Though concerned that the girl's arrival back home would not go unnoticed, Forrester doubted she would betray their trust. His only worry was what they would do once they reached the mouth of the cave. Jonah seemed content to follow his orders and had not challenged Forrester's assertion that they would explore the caverns together. If what the girl had said was true, he would need the hunchback's assistance to translate for him when he came face to face with those who dwelt within the depths.

They finished their cigarettes and clambered to their feet. Forrester nodded to Jonah and they hurried back in the direction of the cottage. Rather than approach directly, they skirted around it and headed as quietly as possible back to the cove where they had beached the day before.

Once there, Jonah untied the boat from its mooring and they hauled it into the water. The waves on this side of the island did not seem as calm as on the eastern side and they struggled to pull the boat out far enough before the next wave pushed it back towards the shore. After wrestling against the tide for a number of minutes they were able to climb in and Jonah began to row them out to where they could raise the sail. As the hunchback hauled on the lines to raise the sail, Forrester spotted something on the horizon that froze his blood.

"Those sails," he murmured, "I recognise them."

Jonah grabbed hold of the mast to steady himself and peered across the sea at the approaching boat.

"The Manannán!" he hissed. "It's Macleod!"

Jonah shoved Forrester to the thwarts and yanked on the lines attached to the sail.

"Sit yerself!" he yelled. "An' watch your head on the boom."

Forrester ducked as the wind filled the sail and the boom swung inches above his head. Jonah held the lines in a clenched fist and pulled on the tiller with his other hand. The small boat lurched as the wind thrashed them into the open water and into the path of the Manannán.

"What are you doing?" Forrester yelled.

"Jonah's no' goin' tae risk sailin' close tae the shore," the hunchback answered through gritted teeth. "He'd sooner take his chances wi' Macleod an' his boys than the rocks."

Forrester clung to the gunwale as the boat skipped over the white-crested waves. He turned in his seat to see the vast sails of the Manannán looming behind them.

"They're gaining on us!" he groaned. "Is there any way of going any faster?"

"Aye. If the English was tae step out, he'd be lightenin' the load. I'm sure we'd be gettin' a few more knots, no' tae mention some peace an' quiet."

"That's not funny," Forrester snapped.

"Daes he see Jonah laughin'?"

Though the canvas sail was stretched taut in the wind and Jonah was doing all he could to coax more speed out of the small boat, it was evident to Forrester that their flight would be short-lived. With each minute that passed the imposing bulk of Macleod's boat drew closer and Forrester's sense of dread grew.

Jonah cast a quick glance over his deformed shoulders and swore. He sighed with resignation and pushed the tiller away from him whilst tightening his grip on the lines. The boom swung outwards and the boat veered to one side.

"What the bloody hell are you doing now?" Forrester roared. "We're headed right for them!"

"There's no' a chance o' this tub outrunnin' a Zulu. The only advantage we have is tae jib intae the wind an' hope the bastards cannae turn so fast."

Forrester sat low in the boat as Jonah sailed them into the wind, the boom swinging from side to side as they snaked across the path of the larger vessel. Angry voices carried over the water and the figures on the Zulu shook their fists and gesticulated wildly as they saw the manoeuvre.

The gamble paid off. Though the crew of the Zulu reacted quickly there was no way the cumbersome craft could match the agility of the small skiff. The distance between the boats widened and Forrester allowed himself a sigh of relief when he saw Jonah's victorious smile.

"Good show," he exclaimed joyously. "You certainly showed them."

Jonah winked as the boom swung across once more and he pulled the lines taut.

"Aye, good enough but Macleod's a canny sailor an' willnae fall for that a second time. He's turned the now, see? We may have a wee distance between us but I daresay we'll no' be able tae keep 'em away long."

A gunshot rang out and echoed across the open water. Both Jonah and Forrester ducked their heads instinctively as a bullet splintered part of the gunwale.

"Stay as low as you can," Forrester yelled. "They've got rifles."

"Jimmy Munro won't be best pleased wi' that," Jonah replied as a second shot whizzed above their heads and punched a neat hole through the sail.

"What do we do now?"

"There's a choice. We could lead 'em further out ontae the Galtachean, the rocks in the west, but that's some distance an' if we cannae keep 'em away they'll catch us in open water an' feed us tae the fish."

"What's the other option?"

Jonah pointed to the coastline of Garbh Eilean that rose out of the foaming waters on their left hand side.

"We try an' beach on the rough island then find some way tae fight them on land."

Forrester looked from the billowing sea on their right to the towering cliffs on their left.

"That's not much of a choice."

"Aye," Jonah frowned. "Either way we're headed for rocks an' that disnae bode well for this wee boat. Can he swim?"

"I'd rather not have to."

"That settles it then," Jonah grimaced and steered towards land. "This way, he'll only have tae swim a wee bit."

The deck of the Manannán seethed with activity as its crew saw what their prey was planning. Knowing that the boat would stand no chance against the solid rocks, the Zulu pursued the skiff no closer to the shore.

"That should gi' us chust enough time tae find good cover," Jonah stated flatly. "But they'll find a way ontae the island no bother."

Forrester grunted a noncommittal response and gripped the gunwale as the boat rose and fell on the waves. His eyes scanned the shore towards which they were headed but could see no suitable places to disembark, just foaming white waters and the glistening black rocks lurking beneath. The cliffs were steep and rose for dozens of feet at the lowest points. Scaling them with rope and harness would have been exhausting and Forrester found himself trembling at the prospect of attempting such a climb without equipment.

"That other plan," he began, his voice cracking with fear, "perhaps I was a mite hasty in dismissing it."

"Too late," Jonah cried as the boat was lifted by another wave and thrown onto the rocks.

The impact was jarring and despite his firm grip, Forrester was torn from his seat and thrown into the freezing waters.

The force of the waves turned him over and over, leaving him so disorientated he no longer knew which way was up. Panicking, he opened his mouth to yell and felt a torrent cascade into his throat. Choking and flailing helplessly, his body was caught by the merciless waves and slammed against a partially submerged rock. Feeling the current begin to drag him back beneath the surface, he clung on, heaving and retching to rid his lungs of brine.

The boat itself had been ruptured by the collision with the rocks and had broken apart with the battering of the waves. Jonah had managed to brace himself for the initial blow but soon the relentless pounding caused him to slip into the sea. He scrambled with frantic movements until his feet touched the bottom and he knew he had reached the shallows. He staggered on, thrown off-balance by the uneven surface beneath his feet and the perpetual drag of the water.

Peering through the spray, Jonah could see Forrester clinging for dear life to a nearby rock. He could not make out the Englishman's words over the roaring of the sea but could see that he was in some distress. Having waded over, he reached out and grabbed him around the neck. Forrester struggled at first, still confused by his immersion in the depths. He fought his way free from Jonah's grip and strove to return to the relative safety of the rock. Jonah eventually succeeded and was able to pull Forrester onto the slippery shelf of rock at the foot of the cliffs. There they lay side by side, coughing and spluttering as the sea continued to rage around them.

"That went well," Forrester gasped.

"No' bad," Jonah agreed, wringing the water from his clothes.

They watched the Manannán swing about so that the huge sail caught the full brunt of the wind. The Zulu flashed across the waves and was soon little more than a speck on the horizon. Though shaken, Forrester knew that time was short and began studying the rock face for the easiest route to the top. Jonah stood by his side and straightened himself as much as his crooked spine would allow.

"A long way tae the top," he commented.

"I can't see any other way."

"It would be best if the English went first," Jonah gestured with a hand.

The climb was tortuous. Whilst pitted with hand holds, the craggy face of the cliff was almost vertical. Already tired from their battle to extricate themselves from the seething tide, their ascent was made no easier by their sodden clothes. On several occasions rocks that had seemed stable enough to support their weight would crumble and leave them fumbling for purchase against the bare stone.

The pain in Forrester's forearms started when he had covered less than a third of the climb. By the time he had struggled halfway up the cliff the pain had spread to his shoulders. The final few feet were the most draining as he found himself barely able to move his fingertips enough to maintain a firm hold on the rocks. Gritting his teeth against the agony in his fatigued muscles, Forrester somehow found the reserves of strength to heave himself onto the top of the cliff. Jonah followed shortly behind, rolling onto his back and groaning.

"It didnae seem so tall from the bottom."

They did not rest for long and were soon on their feet, their eyes searching the rugged terrain before them for some form of cover from the impending attack.

"Daes the English have any plans?" Jonah asked.

"Nothing springs to mind at the moment," Forrester answered. "Our best bet looks to be that ruin over there."

Jonah's eyes followed Forrester's outstretched arm until they fixed on a crumbling drystone wall a few hundred yards away. He nodded his assent and began the climb up the slope to where it lay. Forrester's heart sank a little lower as they drew closer to the stones. It was a blackhouse, or at least it had been a blackhouse before time and the elements had their way with the structure. The roof had fallen in and many of the heavy stones that comprised the walls had been removed long ago, leaving only two sides of the building behind which they might hide themselves.

"This is no good," Forrester groaned. "We'd be fine if they were to come from the same direction as we did but if they were to come from the other side we'd have no cover whatsoever."

Jonah did not answer him but kicked a loose rock with the toe of his boot. Forrester climbed onto the wall and glanced at the bare surroundings.

"Nothing," he spat. "Nothing but mud, heather and rocks."

"Jonah's guessin' we'll be stayin' here then?"

Forrester jumped down and began shifting some of the smaller rocks to build a small defensive wall. Seeing Forrester's plan, Jonah needed no prompting and set to the lifting. They worked quickly, exchanging few words as they built the barricade. By the time they finished the two main walls had shrunk in height by about a foot but they had been able to construct an adequate fortification behind which they could crouch should Macleod and his men attempt to attack from the rear.

Their defences built, Forrester took apart his revolver, cleaning and checking the mechanisms were in working order after their soaking. Jonah searched the area for any small stones he could use as a projectile and gave a bark of triumph when he found an old but sturdy timber with a cruel-looking nail sticking out of one side. He swung the cudgel a few times at imaginary foes before sitting down with his back to the wall, seemingly satisfied with his makeshift arsenal.

"Got a smoke?" he asked.

Forrester shook his head. He reached into his pocket and removed the cigarette case. Opening it, he showed Jonah the sodden remnants of the few remaining cigarettes.

"There'll be no last cigarette," Forrester sighed. "At least Macleod doesn't know where we are. We still have the element of surprise."

"Shite," Jonah grumbled. "There's no' that many places tae hide. Full well Macleod kens where we are. The bastard's chust toyin' wi' us. What a way tae die... an' no' a cigarette tae ease the passin' o' time."

"We're not dead yet," Forrester barked, waving the revolver beneath Jonah's nose. "I'm not planning on going down without a fight."

"That's chust what Jonah was afraid of."

They watched the surroundings and waited. Though their bodies were exhausted from the sleepless night and the day's exertions, their minds and eyes remained sharp. Nothing escaped their keen gaze. The wind brushed the heather-covered slopes and whistled through the cracks of the walls. Occasionally, a fulmar would be disturbed from its nest and then burst into the air, its cry shattering the stillness.

The waiting irritated Forrester. He cursed their situation and chewed anxiously on his lower lip until he tasted blood. The sun climbed to its highest point and had begun its slow descent by the time Jonah pointed to the figure creeping through the heather towards them.

Forrester signalled that they should remain quiet and they ducked out of sight. The man walked carefully, crouching low to keep his body close to the ground. He was dressed in a coarse woollen coat and a pair of ragged trousers. His feet were bare and he carried what appeared to be an old flintlock rifle. Forrester studied the man's movements for a while before he ducked back behind the wall.

"He's not seen us yet," he whispered, fearful that even a quiet word would carry on the breeze. "But he's armed and I'm guessing he isn't alone. As soon as the first shot is fired his chums will know exactly where we are and the game is up. Our best bet is to draw him near and try to get the rifle from him."

"An' how will we dae that?"

"He's got an old rifle, a muzzle-loader. He's not going to risk a shot unless he's certain he won't miss. I want you to stand up and get his attention. He'll try and come closer before he takes his shot."

"An' if he disnae?"

"Then you're having a bad day."

"What if the Englishman misses his shot?"

"Then we're both having a bad day."

Jonah wrinkled his lip, torn between terror and amusement. He shrugged once and clambered to his feet. He vaulted the wall with surprising agility and sprinted as best he could away from the ruins.

The man spotted him immediately and raised his rifle. Forrester held his breath as he watched the man attempt to draw a bead on the moving target. He exhaled with relief when the man shook his head and set off in pursuit. Though the hunchback did not run quickly, he bobbed and weaved, changing direction enough to make it hard for the hunter to take a clear shot.

Forrester smiled as the man came closer to his hiding place. He was young, barely in his twenties, and gripped the rifle as though fearful he might drop it. His attention was fixed on the fleeing figure and did not see Forrester until it was too late.

The young man's jaw fell open when Forrester emerged from behind the shelter. He began to raise the rifle to his shoulder but was too slow. The Webley Boxer in Forrester's hands roared and the bullet struck the young man just above the heart. He staggered backwards, blinking dumbly. He tried to hold the rifle steady but his arms failed him and it fell to the ground. The young man threw his head back as if to scream but the only sound to escape his lips was a low gurgle before he collapsed onto the soft heather.

The gunshot had echoed around the small island. Upon hearing it, Jonah had stopped in his tracks to check that he was unharmed. Realising that the shot had come from Forrester's pistol, he turned and headed back to the ruined blackhouse.

Jonah found Forrester standing over the body of the young man. He approached wordlessly but Forrester heard his clumsy steps and turned. His face was flushed, beads of sweat hung on his brow and his eyes gleamed with an intensity that Jonah found unsettling.

"Is he dead?"

Forrester grunted and bent down to retrieve the young man's rifle. Having handed the weapon to Jonah, he searched the body for gunpowder and shot.

"We'd best head back to the wall," he said, his voice devoid of emotion. "Macleod can't have missed that racket and will be headed straight here."

With that, he turned and began striding back up the slope that led to their barricade. Jonah took one last look at the body and felt his stomach turn. As he followed Forrester, he found himself thinking about the fire he had seen in the Englishman's eyes.

"And they call Jonah mad," he muttered.

Chapter 13

Crouching behind the ruined walls, Jonah searched the landscape of the rough island for any sign of Macleod and his men. He gripped the flintlock rifle they had taken from the dead man and hoped that his nerves would not affect his aim. Forrester sat beside him in stoic silence. He showed no traces of guilt after the killing and did not seem at all nervous about the imminent attack. Rather, it seemed to Jonah, the Englishman appeared impatient, as though eager for battle to begin.

They had exchanged few words in the past hour. Forrester had shown Jonah how to shoot and reload the ancient firearm and had warned him against wasting shots by firing too hastily. In truth, Jonah very much doubted he would be able to use the weapon with any enthusiasm. He had only fired a gun on a handful of occasions before and even then could not bring himself to kill the rabbits he had been aiming for. The notion of pointing the rifle at another human being filled him with unease.

"Jonah disnae think he can dae this," he muttered.

"You're going to have to," Forrester answered bluntly.

"Killin's a sin," Jonah's voice cracked with anxiety. "Even Jonah kens that."

"It may well be a sin, but I'd rather be alive and sinful than dead and regretful. If we make it through this you'll have plenty of time left to atone for your sins."

"Is that how the Englishman daes it?" Jonah asked. "Is that how he could kill that lad wi'out breakin' a sweat?"

"If I remember rightly, he was aiming for you. Would you rather I had let him live?"

Jonah shook his head and handed the rifle to Forrester.

"It's no' that simple," he sighed.

"Things rarely are," Forrester said as he took the rifle. He lifted it to his shoulder and gazed along the length of the barrel.

"Can you reload for me?"

Jonah nodded hastily, a strange mixture of shame and relief burning within him.

Neither man spoke for a time but it was Forrester who eventually broke the silence.

"In answer to your question, Jonah," he began, "I do it when I know it is the right course of action. I don't enjoy taking a man's life, but if left with no alternative then I'll pull the trigger and lose no sleep over it."

"How many?"

"I beg your pardon?"

"How many has the Englishman killed?"

Forrester ran his hand through his moustache and looked

thoughtful for a moment or two.

"Let's put it this way... If I was the sort to worry about a stain on my soul or whatever, I'd spend every waking moment in prayer. Losing one's faith does have its advantages."

It was another hour before they saw any sign of Macleod or his men. Forrester expressed his surprise when he saw them approach as a group and brought the rifle up ready to fire. He had expected a little more tact from the attackers than a full-frontal assault. With a few choice curses, he thumbed back the hammer of the rifle and closed one eye to take aim, then hesitated.

"What is it?" Jonah asked, his nerves fraught with tension.

"Something's wrong," Forrester hissed. "There's a woman with them."

Jonah shuffled to Forrester's side and peered at the approaching group with dismay.

"Mor Campbell!" he exclaimed, "They've gone an' taken the expectin' lassie!"

The figures drew closer and soon there was no doubt that held in the midst of the four men was the pregnant young woman. She stumbled as she walked though Macleod held her by one arm for support. Forrester's rage grew when he saw that Macleod held an ugly metal spike pointed at her round belly.

Forrester swore and lowered the gun. Of the three men accompanying Macleod, two carried rifles whilst the third wielded a long pole topped with a gaff hook. Four men with just two rifles between them. With their elevated position and crude but sturdy defences, Forrester felt that he and Jonah would have been able to put up some kind of a fight. The presence of the girl changed all that. There would be no exchange of gunfire, no bloodshed. He placed the rifle on the ground and rose to his feet. Jonah muttered an oath in Gaelic and followed him.

The guns of the two armed men were trained on Forrester and Jonah from the moment they stepped out from the cover of the ruined blackhouse. Macleod smiled broadly as he saw that the two men were surrendering themselves without a fight. He pushed Mor Campbell into the arms of the man carrying the gaff and strode forward as if to greet them.

"I can see ye're no' as stupid as ye're reckless," he boomed. "I've ne'er seen a man tempt fate as often as ye."

"If you hadn't been hiding behind a pregnant woman, I'd have shot you on sight," Forrester snarled, his hands balled into fists by his sides.

"Oho!" Macleod laughed. "There's still a wee fight left in him!"

Before Forrester could reply, one of Macleod's huge fists shot out and struck him in the stomach. He doubled over, the wind knocked out of him. Jonah helped him back to his feet and Forrester glared at the burly Scotsman as he fought for breath.

"I'm afraid ye're mistaken if ye think I'd hide behind a gyurl," Macleod taunted. "Mor here was chust as willin' tae help me as the last time we met."

Forrester and Jonah watched with disbelief as Macleod draped one of his powerful arms around the young woman's shoulders and planted a slobbering kiss on her cheek. Mor blushed and smiled at this attention, but pointedly avoided Forrester's gaze.

One of the men reached into his pocket and handed

Macleod a ball of twine. The large man quickly bound the hands of his captives behind their backs and searched through their pockets. He smiled as he removed Forrester's revolver from its place of concealment and waved it at his cronies.

"Would ye look at this, boys?" he crowed. "Quite a fine tool the Inspector carries wi' him."

Jonah watched Forrester's eyes burn with impotent rage as Macleod pocketed the gun. The look did not escape Macleod's notice and he swaggered forward to stand before the Englishman.

"Ye shouldnae be so concerned who takes your belongings. Ye'll be dead soon enough," he gloated.

Forrester's head shot forward and caught the bridge of Macleod's nose with a sickening crunch. Macleod staggered backwards, blood streaming from his nostrils. Bellowing with fury he lashed out and pounded Forrester with his great fists until the Englishman lost his footing and collapsed. Even then, Macleod did not cease his attack, kicking and stamping on the fallen man. Finally satisfied, Macleod stepped back, panting with exhilaration. He towered over Jonah who eyeballed him defiantly but made no sign of aggression. Macleod grunted once then spat at the feet of the hunchback.

"Ye'll no' be any trouble will ye, Crotach?" he sneered.

Jonah gave no answer but cleared his throat noisily and launched a hefty gobbet of phlegm at Macleod's own feet. Macleod grimaced as he looked at his spittle-covered boots then swung a wild punch that connected with Jonah's jaw and lifted him off his feet.

"Drag 'em tae the boat," Macleod barked and set off in the direction of the shore.

***

The cold water lapped against Forrester's chin and roused him from unconsciousness. His body ached from where Macleod's blows had landed but when he attempted to examine his injuries he found his hands were held in place. Turning his head, he saw the ropes that bound his wrists were fastened to a pair of metal hoops driven deep into the rock behind him.

His body and legs hung freely, supported by the water that ebbed around the base of the rock. Jonah was trussed up in a similar manner a few feet away though his crooked back meant that he had been tied facing the rock rather than looking out on the expanse of sea. The hunchback's body hung limply, his head drooping dangerously close to the waters.

Forrester called Jonah's name several times but got no response. He spent some time struggling against his bindings, testing the knots and rope for weaknesses but to no avail. Throwing back his head, he roared with frustration until his throat burned and his lungs were sore. When he felt the tears begin to flow he chastised himself by pounding the back of his head on the rock until his vision blurred.

"What a din!" Jonah called out. "Is the Englishman tryin' tae wake the kraken?"

Hearing the hunchback's voice, Forrester allowed himself to relax and stopped struggling. Jonah had turned to face him and Forrester could see the split lip and bruising where he had been struck.

"Are you alright?" he asked.

"Aye, no' bad. Yerself?" Jonah managed a smile through his

swollen lips. "At least Macleod gave the Englishman a room wi' a view. All Jonah has tae choose from is this rock or his damned ugly face."

"Which is worse?"

"The rock may be prettier, but it's shite for conversation. So I'll stick wi' lookin' at the Englishman."

"Jolly good." Forrester winced as he felt the rope biting into his wrists. "I don't suppose you have any suggestions on how we could free ourselves?"

"None," Jonah scowled. "Jonah was under the impression that the Englishman was the one wi' all the plans. He should ken what tae dae, should he no'?"

"This wasn't exactly part of my plan. I don't know about you but I'm tied firmly here. The only way I'm getting off this rock is if someone was to take a knife to these ropes. Given that it's pretty unlikely anyone will sail close enough to spot us, I'm guessing we're going to starve here."

"Daen't be daft," Jonah spat. "He's no' goin' tae starve. Can he no' see the tide is risin'? He'll drown long before he has the chance tae starve!"

Hearing these words, Forrester resumed his struggling against the ropes and screamed desperate entreaties at the top of his voice until breathless. Jonah watched him with a bemused expression.

"Daes he think that'll work?" he asked after a time.

"It's better than just dangling here waiting to drown," Forrester croaked scornfully. The inspector continued to pull at his bindings, biting his lip against the pain of the rope cutting into his flesh and the ache in his shoulders. It was during this time that Jonah pointed out that the tide had turned against them. The gently lapping waters were becoming waves that grew taller and taller with each passing moment.

"Shouldnae be long now," Jonah sighed.

The waves began to grow in size and ferocity. They broke against the men tied to the rock with exhausting regularity. After swallowing several mouthfuls of water, Forrester was able to establish a pattern for his breathing; holding his breath when submerged and gasping for air when the waves drew back. Though his lungs grew accustomed to this manner of breathing, the time spent with his head beneath the cold water increased with each new wave.

Forrester knew he would not be able to sustain himself for much longer. Soon enough, his head would be swamped by the waves for good. His belaboured lungs would fill with water and douse the flame of life within him. Knowing such thoughts were dangerous, he set his mind on escaping and once more began to tug at the ropes that shackled him to the rock.

His heart leapt when he felt the iron ring on his left hand side turn slightly. He looped what slack rope there was around the ring and pulled with all his might. Sure enough, the ring moved once more. With one final heave that set the muscles in his shoulder afire, the metal spike that held the ring in place came free from the rock. Having taken several deep breaths he started work on the rope around his right hand. The knots were tight and their lengthy immersion in water had only served to make them still harder to untie. Using his chattering teeth and frozen fingers to loosen the knots, he inwardly cursed every second that passed, knowing that whilst time was short for him, it was even shorter for Jonah, who was beginning to struggle against his fetters, his mouth occasionally breaking the surface of the water and spluttering for help.

Finally, the knots loosened and Forrester slipped his hand

out of the rope. He paddled over to where Jonah hung and examined his restraints. As Jonah had fought against his bindings far less, the knots had not been pulled so tight and were substantially easier to untie. Once released, Jonah threw his arms around Forrester's neck and planted a slobbering kiss on his forehead.

"Jonah ne'er thought he'd kiss an Englishman!" he roared.

"A firm handshake and a 'thank you' would have sufficed," Forrester responded drily.

Together, they clambered further up the rock and surveyed their surroundings.

"That's Garbh Eilean there," Jonah pointed at the familiar landmass. "This rock must be one o' the Galtachean. A fine place tae leave us, doubtless. He saw how fast the waters change hereabouts. A sailor'd have tae be lost or plain mad tae come within a hundred yards o' them."

"Should we swim for the shore?" Forrester asked.

"Jonah would sooner stick hot coals up his arse. The waters 'tween this rock an' the rough island are pure treacherous. The tide'd drag even the strongest swimmer out intae the Minch. The best he could hope for would be tae wash up on a beach in Harris so that he can be given a proper Christian burial."

"You fill me with confidence." Forrester winced as he examined his wrists that had been left ugly and raw by the chafing ropes. "What do you suggest we do?"

"No' a thing. Chust sit here an' wait."

"For what?"

"Jonah reckons those friends o' Macleod's will be payin' a visit shortly. They'll finish the Englishman," Jonah said, peering down at the fathomless depths around them and shivering, "if he disnae freeze tae death first."

Forrester joined Jonah in gazing into the deep and groaned. The hunchback was right, their situation was hopeless. Perhaps it would have been just as well not to have bothered freeing themselves from the ropes and suffering the quick death in the sea rather than the long, drawn out fate they now faced. He let his weary head sink into his hands and shuddered with exhaustion. He was uncertain exactly how long he remained in this position but when he next lifted his head, the sun was sinking beneath the horizon and the purple twilight was spreading across the Minch.

"How long have I been sleeping?" he croaked, his throat parched.

"A few hours," Jonah answered, without taking his eyes off the dark shape of the island before them.

"What are you looking at?"

Jonah raised a trembling hand and pointed. Forrester followed the finger but at first could not make anything out in the fading light. However, after a few moments he spotted what Jonah had been looking at. There was a small sail approaching them. The rolling waves occasionally obscured it from view but his eyes remained fixed on the spot and he felt a surge of relief at this glimmer of hope.

"It's not Macleod!" he grinned.

"Aye. That much he can be thankful for. Jonah disnae recognise the sail. It's a wee boat, that much I ken."

They watched with growing anticipation as the boat drew closer. They could distinguish two figures sitting in its bows, huddled against the cold wind that drove them towards the rocks. Jonah and Forrester stiffly pushed themselves to their feet to wave and holler at the approaching vessel. The smaller of the two figures returned the wave and the small boat tacked in their direction.

"That was a woman!" Forrester exclaimed.

"Aye, it was. An' Jonah recognises the big cove on the tiller. It's the balabhan an' one o' the lassies."

"I can only hope that she's Catriona and not that deceitful slut Mor."

The boat came closer and both Jonah and Forrester breathed a sigh of relief as they saw Catriona's unmistakable fair curls dancing in the wind. When the boat was a dozen yards from the rock Catriona cupped her hands to her mouth and called out.

"Are ye hurt?"

"Not badly," Forrester replied. "It's good to see a friendly face."

"We cannae bring the boat any closer tae the rocks," she yelled. "Can ye swim over here?"

Needing no further encouragement, Jonah and Forrester plunged back into the water and paddled over to the waiting boat. John Campbell offered one of his enormous hands and helped haul Jonah aboard. Forrester clung to the side and waited for his turn to clamber onboard. John reached down and grasped him by the forearm but as he did so, Forrester felt a weight around his legs pulling him back into the water.

"Something's got me!" he shrieked, feeling the grip around his legs tighten.

Jonah and Catriona scrambled to grasp Forrester's other

arm as he began to lose his grip on the gunwale. A sudden tug took them all by surprise and the boat pitched wildly from side to side. Forrester's yells became more strident and he kicked out at whatever was trying to pull him into the depths. His foot struck something solid and he felt the hold on his legs loosen momentarily. Those in the boat fell backwards as Forrester was jerked from the sea and landed in a sodden heap on top of them.

A nightmarish head burst from the depths, its sudden appearance instigating a terrified cry from Catriona Campbell. Rivulets of water ran off the creature's smooth grey skin. Large yellow eyes peered at them with interest. Two narrow slits that served as nostrils flared as it sniffed the air before the cavernous mouth opened to reveal rows of tiny, pointed teeth. The creature hissed at the those in the boat before it sank beneath the waves as quickly as it had appeared and was seen no more.

"What the bloody hell was that?" Forrester wheezed, joining the others who cautiously peered over the side into the churning waters.

"It's time we were goin'," Catriona whimpered. "Where there's one there's sure tae be others."

Forrester offered no argument and slumped against the thwarts of the boat. He took a deep breath and allowed his heavy eyelids to droop. Though he knew that they were by no means clear of danger, he could not fight the overwhelming sense of exhaustion. The gentle rocking of the boat soothed him and loosened his grip on consciousness. Unable to fight any longer, his eyes closed and he drifted off into a deep slumber.

Chapter 14

His vision was blurred when he first attempted to open his eyes. Indistinct shapes shifted into the shadows. Gradually, he was able to pick out familiar objects; a dresser, a chair, a fireplace. His mind moved sluggishly. He realised he was in a room but did not recognise it. It was not his room at the Royal Hotel, nor did it appear to be the Campbells' small house on Eilean an Tigh. On a nearby bed lay a body huddled under blankets. The covers rose and fell in time with the steady snoring emanating from beneath them.

The room was small and dimly lit. A tattered piece of cloth hung in front of an small window that was left ajar and the makeshift curtain flapped with the gentle breeze. The walls were bare, the crumbling brickwork blackened with soot. A strong smell of fish seemed to permeate everything in the room, from the coarse straw mats on the floor to the blankets on his bed.

Forrester tried to rise but was quickly overcome with dizziness and fell back onto the bed with a groan. It was then that he noticed his clothes had been removed. He groaned once more as he examined the numerous cuts and grazes that covered his body. A bandage was wrapped tightly around his chest and a dull throbbing told him that the worst of the abrasions were on his back. The skin on the palms of his hands bore testament to his ordeal, a multitude of shallow cuts giving them a scoured appearance and making the smallest movements of his digits a tortuous challenge.

"The barnacles," a voice spoke.

Forrester glanced up from his injured hands and saw Jonah smiling at him from the other bed.

"The barnacles," Jonah repeated. "Those rocks must've been covered in the wee bastards. Ye dinnae notice 'em when ye're in the water. That blone Effie was sayin' the Englishman's back looks as though he's been flayed alive."

"That would explain the bandages," Forrester shifted his weight carefully to sit up straight. "But how did we come to be here?"

"That Campbell gyurl an' the balabhan, they took us off that rock. Daes he no' recall? Twas fine timin' on their part an' all. If they'd been a few moments later we'd be floatin' in the Minch wi' Macleod's strange friends!"

"I don't remember the journey back here," Forrester said, his fingers tentatively probing the bruises on the back of his head.

"Aye, well, he wouldnae. The Englishman fell intae a faint nae sooner than he got in the boat. By the time Stornoway was gained he was ravin' wi' fever an' babblin' all kinds o' nonsense about the great absolute or somethin'. Twas a stroke o' luck that Effie was down on the quay when we arrived. She had us brought here an' wouldnae hear o' callin' for Doctor Murray. A good job an' all - If Murdo Macleod heard we'd got off that rock he'd be beatin' on that door tae finish the job himself."

"How long have we been here?"

"Jonah's no' so sure himself but it must be a couple o' days."

"Where is Effie now? How is she?"

"Och, the gyurl's better than the last time he saw her. A wee bit bruised but she's back out at the farlins an' the fish. It's gettin' late, she'll no' be long."

When Effie entered the small room, she pulled off her apron and the protective bindings on her fingers and set about tending to her patients. She bathed their wounds with warm water, changed their bandages and prepared a light meal of smoked fish and boiled potatoes for the three of them.

Forrester watched her as she stood by the cooking pots and was pleased to see that the bruises on her face were beginning to fade. They ate in silence, their gratitude best expressed by their clean plates and satisfied smiles. Effie seemed uncomfortable with the lack of conversation and occupied herself by shovelling more coals onto the fire before settling into the rocking chair that sat before it.

"It's time ye left," she said, her eyes fixed on the dancing flames in the hearth.

"We are both indebted to you for all this, Effie," Forrester responded. "Without your hospitality I don't know what we would have done."

"Not here," she snapped. "I didnae mean ye should leave this room. I mean Stornoway. Ye should leave the island, both of ye, while ye still can."

"But I'm not finished here."

"Yes, ye are," she retorted, her eyes reflecting the flames she stared at.

"But Macleod-"

"Tae hell wi' Macleod!" she yelled. "Tae hell wi' his boats an' his whisky an' all the herring in the Minch! D'ye no' see that ye cannae win? Even if ye were tae find out for certain that he killed Colin McCormick an' the Mackinnon lad, even then what difference would it make? What could ye dae tae him? He's a big man here an' regardless of your good intentions ye're chust another Englishman; far from home an' way out o' your depth!"

Silenced by her anger, Forrester lowered his gaze. He heard Jonah clamber from his bed and exchange muffled words with Effie who was sobbing into her hands.

"You're right," Forrester said after a time.

Effie looked up, her face streaked with tears.

"D'ye mean ye'll leave?" she asked.

"No." A gentle smile softened his features. "You're right about me, but I'm not leaving. Not until I've finished with Macleod."

"He came damned close tae killin' ye both last time ye met," Effie whispered. "What makes ye think he won't succeed next time?"

"He might," Forrester shrugged. "I won't deny he's a dangerous man. But we know more about his strange friends now. What Mor Campbell told us about her father and the Blue Men got me thinking. Big Donald Campbell struck up a deal with those things so that his family would be left in peace.

They aren't mindless animals, they can be reasoned with. Murdo Macleod knows this and he doesn't want anyone else to find out his secret. He didn't leave us tied to that rock expecting the tide to kill us, he wanted those things to do his dirty work for him. Macleod has got some kind of control over them. I think they allow his boats to fish the Sound of Shiant in exchange for bottles of his whisky but I doubt they have any real idea of his plans. I intend to tell them."

"What makes ye think ye can reason wi' the Blue Men?" Effie sniffed.

"The Englishman can be gey persuasive when he wants tae be," Jonah said, placing a reassuring arm around her shoulders.

"I'll need your help, Jonah."

"Jonah's always happy tae help," the hunchback winked. "But ye're forgettin' one thing. How daes he propose tae get back out tae the Shiants? After what we did tae Jimmy Munro's skiff, Jonah disnae reckon they'll find another fisherman from here tae Lochmaddy that'd lend their boat."

"We'll just have to take one," Forrester ran a hand over the stubble on his chin. "I'm sure Murdo Macleod has one going spare."

Effie shrugged off Jonah's arm and began to clear away the empty dinner plates. The men watched as she busied herself in the small room, clearly struggling with her emotions. After washing and drying the plates, she placed them beside the pots and pans that were gathered by the hearth. This done, she could contain herself no longer and the tears once more began to trickle down her pale cheeks.

"Bleedin' men," she sobbed. "It's ne'er enough wi' ye, is it? Ye cannae chust walk away an' let people get on wi' their lives. Dae my feelings mean so little tae ye, Edmund? D'ye no' care that there are people worryin' about ye? Macleod beat me sure enough an' the two of ye run off an' near get yourselves killed. An' for what, I ask ye? If ye go out there again, I willnae be here tae patch ye up if ye come back."

With these words she stormed out of the room, slamming the door behind her with such force that one of the plates she had so carefully placed by the hearth toppled over and smashed. Forrester and Jonah looked at one another but said nothing, knowing mere words would do nothing to change the path on which they were now set.

***

Murdo Macleod owned an apartment at the top of a crowded tenement building overlooking North Beach. He did not call these rooms home but both he and his crew used them for drinking and gambling and whoring. As was to be expected from rooms used for such a purpose, the apartment was sparsely furnished. Miscellaneous fishing tackle littered the floors. Coils of frayed rope, broken crates and barrels served as crude furniture. Hemp sackcloth nailed above windows performed the role of curtains to block out the icy wind and rain that blew through the cracked glass panes. The walls were decorated with drunkenly scrawled obscenities and smeared with all manner of filth.

The squalor of the rooms matched the wretched state of those who slumbered in them that night. Macleod's celebrations had started shortly after their return to Stornoway, three days previously. The preceding days and hours had been spent drinking and carousing in the waterfront pubs and when the landlords stopped serving drinks past midnight on the

Sabbath, the party had moved to Macleod's rooms. Songs had been sung, bottles smashed, intoxicated punches thrown and apologies made alongside slobbering endearments of friendship. In short, the men had behaved like animals and now slept like them, curled in corners beneath scraps of blankets or slumped where they sat when they slipped out of consciousness into a deep, whisky-soaked slumber.

The first signs of dawn were beginning to creep into the room. Dim grey light filtered through the makeshift curtains and raised voices from the street below grew in volume until one of the sleeping men awoke, stumbled to the window and gazed out.

The sight that greeted Jack Macphail's bleary eyes was so shocking that he immediately scurried over to where Macleod lay and attempted to rouse the large man. Macleod lay on his back, one arm cradling a half-empty bottle, the other draped over a sleeping whore. Macphail's entreaties finally pierced the veil of unconsciousness and Macleod followed him to the window, muttering a stream of curses at being so rudely awakened.

Leaning out of the window into the cold morning air, Macleod gazed at the crowds swarming around the quayside. He was initially surprised to see such a large gathering of people so early on the Sabbath and was curious to see what had brought them together. His eyes were drawn to a vast plume of smoke that billowed into the sky from what appeared to be a huge floating bonfire. The flaming mass seemed so out of place in the harbour that it took a few moments for Macleod to come to terms with what he saw.

"The boats!" he screamed in alarm. "The bloody boats are burnin'!"

His cries woke the other men in the room and they leapt to

their feet to join him by the window.

Down by the waterfront the crowd watched the blazing vessels with slack jaws and high spirits. It was clear that the fire had been deliberate as only the boats belonging to Murdo Macleod had been targeted. The dampness of the early morning air prevented the flames spreading to the other boats and the empty tar buckets that lay on the beach hinted as to why the fires burned with such ferocity. Nobody made any effort to extinguish the burning boats. Years of enduring the cruelty of Macleod and his thugs left the people of Stornoway indifferent to his current plight.

Macleod and his entourage elbowed their way to the water's edge and the spectators watched with wry amusement as the large man bellowed with inarticulate rage. The fire gave no indication of dying out and a small cheer went up when the flaming mast of the Manannán broke in half and fell into the shallows. Half-submerged, the burnt wood hissed and spat glowing embers that drifted high above the heads of the onlookers.

Macleod fought back tears as he watched the paintwork smoulder and flake off the sides of the boat. Jack Macphail and the other members of the crew stood by their captain and watched helplessly as their livelihood was engulfed by the dancing flames.

"Whoever is responsible for this," Macleod fumed, "I want them found an' I want them dead, d'ye hear?"

Macphail stood by his side, silently counting the burning boats.

"There's one missing," he said, having checked the numbers a second time. "The wee Skaffie's no' there!"

Macleod snapped out of his grim contemplation and turned

to face Macphail.

"What's that ye say?" he growled.

"The Skaffie," Macphail spluttered. "The Skua, she's no' one o' the boats aflame."

Macleod lifted his head and watched the winter breeze carry the black smoke across the waters of the harbour. Fat white gulls wheeled in the sky, crying out in alarm as they swooped past the dark, heavy cloud. Macleod's eyes finally settled on the small grey sail heading out of the safety of the harbour into the open waters of the Minch.

"There she is," he raised a trembling finger to point at the boat as she crept towards the distant horizon.

Macphail raised a hand to his brows and squinted in the early morning light.

"Are ye sure?" he asked. "It's too far out tae see clear. Could it no' be another?"

"That's the Skua," Macleod intoned, "I'd recognise that old sail anywhere."

"What d'ye plan tae dae?"

"Get me a boat," Macleod spat, "I don't care whose. We're goin' after the bastards who did this."

Chapter 15

Forrester adjusted the scarf around his neck in an attempt to block the icy wind which stung his bare skin. Though uncomfortable, such a wind had its advantages. The sail above their heads billowed outwards as the small boat scudded across the white-flecked waves.

Jonah sat at the stern of the boat, one hand gripping the tiller, the other holding a small brass compass which he checked at regular intervals. No sooner had they left the shelter of the harbour did the boat encounter the thick grey mist that blanketed the coastline that morning. Sitting at the bow of the vessel, Forrester peered into the haziness, his eyes searching the waters ahead for any obstructions which might prove hazardous.

"This is madness," he hissed, "I can't see a bloody thing. We'd best turn back, we're going to get ourselves killed!"

Jonah threw his head back and chortled, his laughter echoing about the surrounding emptiness.

"Jonah disnae ken whether the Englishman is brave or

stupid. Turn back, he says! If Jonah was tae turn back the now we'd definitely find ourselves dead men. Burnin' Macleod's boats took some nerve but Jonah has nae doubt he'll be followin' us an' willnae be satisfied till he has our heads mounted on his wall."

"But how can we hope to find the islands in this fog?"

"This is no' fog, man!" Jonah guffawed. "A wee bit o' mornin' mist is all. Chust like an Englishman tae think a mist is a fog. He should see the haar when it rolls in through Broad Bay if he wishes tae see a real fog. As thick as porridge it is an' a boat lost in that is a boat doomed tae gae in circles till it lifts. He shouldnae be worryin' about a wee mist, not when Jonah has his compass."

Forrester clambered back to the stern and looked at the compass over Jonah's shoulder. The brass case had clearly seen better days, being so dented it was barely possible to close. The compass needle trembled slightly with each rise and fall of the boat but mercifully appeared to be holding its direction.

"It looks old," Forrester commented, a little anxious in placing his trust in such an ancient looking artefact. "Have you had it long?"

"No' long," Jonah shook his head and smiled. "Half an hour tae tell the truth. Jonah found it under the seat here. A fair stroke o' good fortune that."

"Does it even work properly?" Forrester balked.

"Jonah certainly hopes so," the hunchback winked. "We'd be mad tae be sailin' the Minch wi' a broken compass, would we no'?"

Not sharing Jonah's mirth at their situation, Forrester moved back to the bow and resumed his fruitless vigil. Time passed without conversation, the only sounds being the rolling of the ceaseless waves and the occasional cry of an airborne gull in search of food. Eventually, the mist began to lift and Forrester's spirits were raised as the dark shapes of the Shiant isles emerged from the indistinct horizon.

"The compass served Jonah well," the hunchback grinned, snapping the brass case shut before slipping it into his pocket. "What daes the Englishman have planned the now?"

"We find the Blue Men," Forrester answered, not taking his gaze off the tall cliffs of the islands.

"And what of Macleod? He'll be in a fair rage, that's certain. Boat or none, him an' his boys'll be out for blood. Jonah would no' be surprised tae see them swimmin' after us like the sharks they are!"

"I always intended for him to follow us," Forrester spoke slowly, his grim determination shaping each word carefully. "The important thing is that we get there before he does."

"And what then? What daes he have planned when face tae face wi' Macleod an' his friends? Jonah doubts he's the sort tae accept an apology. If ye're plannin' on fightin' the man, chust remember he's in possession o' that fancy pistol o' yours."

"There will be no fighting," Forrester stated. "There are other ways to deal with this situation."

"Very well," Jonah smirked as he grasped a vicious-looking marlin spike and took a few experimental jabs with it. "Jonah plans on takin' this wi' him, chust in case the Englishman proves tae be full o' shite."

The boat drew closer to the islands and skirted the rocky north face of Garbh Eilean. Jonah guided the boat across the channel separating the larger islands from Eilean Mhuire and headed for the towering cliffs of the smaller island. The cave of which Mor Campbell had spoken was not difficult to locate. The tide was low and the vast mouth of the cave yawned open several feet above the waterline. Together they lowered the sail and used the oars to scull the boat into the gaping maw.

Inside, the cavern stretched into the darkness and the splashing of their oars seemed magnified by the eerie stillness. Large droplets of water clung to the stalactites hanging above them, occasionally plummeting to break the smooth surface of the water with a resounding splash. Further and further they rowed into the gloom, their eyes gradually adjusting to the dim light. The water reflected the light that crept in through the entrance and strange patterns danced across the rocks around them. A movement into the shadows caught their attention and they glimpsed an agile figure scramble onto a rock ledge at the far end of the cave. They froze as the figure turned its head to gaze at them.

"Is that... Is that one of them?" Forrester whispered.

"Jonah cannae be sure," the hunchback answered. "Whatever it is, it has taken an interest in us."

The creature hissed once and launched itself off the ledge, the slender form barely causing a ripple when it broke the surface of the black water. They waited breathlessly for any sign of it resurfacing but soon realised the creature was not going to reappear.

"Gone," Forrester sighed. "And with it goes our element of surprise."

"At least we can be sure that Campbell blone was tellin' the truth," Jonah shrugged. "There must be a way tae get tae their nest under the water."

They paddled to the spot where the figure had vanished and

began to strip off their clothes, leaving on their long undergarments in the name of decency.

"At least the water's no' deep," Jonah commented once he had dropped the boat's small anchor.

"You stay with the boat until I find the way that thing went," Forrester said before leaving the relative safety of the boat and lowering himself into the water.

Having taken a deep breath he dove beneath the surface and commenced his search for the submerged entrance. He came back up for air three times before finally resurfacing with a grim smile on his face.

"He found it, eh?" Jonah clapped his hands and shrugged off the remainder of his clothes until he stood in the boat wearing only his stained and threadbare underclothes. He slipped into the water beside Forrester and muttered curses through chattering teeth.

"Och! He didnae tell Jonah it was so cold!"

"The cold is the least of our worries." Forrester paddled closer so he could lower his voice, hoping Jonah would do the same. "There's a kind of tunnel about five feet down on that far wall. It's the only way that thing could have gone unless it swam under the boat and straight out the cave."

"Could he see anythin'?"

"Not a thing. It's pitch black down there. The tunnel is narrow – just wide enough to admit one body at a time. Once we're inside, there'll be no turning back. We'll just have to follow it wherever it leads."

"An' if it leads tae nothin'?"

"We drown." Forrester's expression betrayed no emotion as

he spoke. "And our bodies will never be found."

Jonah gave no response to Forrester's words but the fear could be seen written plainly on his ashen face. They shivered as they swam over to the point Forrester had indicated, taking deep breaths in preparation for their long dive into the unknown. When he was ready, Forrester nodded to Jonah then vanished beneath the surface and kicked towards the tunnel mouth.

Swimming blindly in the darkness, he felt his way along the narrow passage, his legs pumping frantically to propel himself towards the exit he so desperately hoped to find. His chest throbbed with the exertion and he allowed a steady stream of bubbles to leave his mouth as he pushed himself further into the tunnel, deeper into the heart of the island.

The darkness was absolute and the gradual incline meant that his bare back scraped against the cold, rough rock of the tunnel's ceiling. Suddenly, he became aware of a pale blue light ahead of him.

Though his lungs were burning he thrust onwards towards the eerie glow. It was with some exultation that he emerged from the confines of the narrow passage and into an open body of water.

Assuming that the blue light indicated the surface, Forrester paddled on towards it. By now he had exhaled the contents of his lungs and could feel the hollow agony as his body screamed out for air. His movements became jerky and erratic as he grew more and more concerned that he would never breathe again. It seemed that no matter how hard he swam, he came no closer to the surface though the light grew brighter and brighter until it was almost dazzling. When he stubbed his fingers on solid rock he realised his mistake. The glow he had been following was not daylight but some kind of phosphorescence of the rocks at the bottom of the pool. Disorientated by the blackness of the tunnel and starved of oxygen, he had swum down instead of up.

Fighting against his rising panic he placed both feet on the glowing rocks and kicked off from them, propelling himself upwards with all his might.

Each stroke he took brought him closer to the surface but also sapped his already depleted strength. His tortured muscles ached as he fought his way through the water and his head pounded with his quickening pulse. Lights began to dance before his eyes yet he knew they were not the gleaming phosphorescent rocks of the pool.

Sensing his body could take little more punishment, he struggled on and broke the surface of the water with an explosive gasp that echoed around the large chamber into which he had emerged. Panting for breath he clawed his way out of the pool and rolled onto his back, unable to do anything but hungrily inhale the stale air of the cave.

A few seconds passed before Jonah burst from the pool and paddled over to Forrester's side.

"Well that was no' fun," he wheezed before collapsing onto the ground, equally drained by his ordeal.

"At least we're both here."

"That disnae make Jonah feel any better. We may be here, but that makes little difference if he disnae ken where here is!"

Forrester pushed himself to his feet and looked around. The deep pool from which they had emerged was surrounded by a floor of loose stones and pebbles. The ceiling was low and the strange glow from the pool filled the chamber with a cold blue light. Other than the rocks that littered the floor, the cavern was cluttered with numerous artefacts that suggested some kind of habitation. To one side was heaped a large pile of discarded fish bones and empty shells. Forrester moved over to the pile and pulled out an empty bottle. More bottles lay amidst a jumble of slimy rope and driftwood that was heaped beside the entrance to another passage leading off into the shadows.

"These boys like a drink, eh?" Jonah whispered. "Which way now?"

"There." Forrester pointed at the drops of water that began by the side of the pool and disappeared into the dark, dank passageway. "The thing must have gone this way."

"Aye, nae doubt it scurried off tae find it's pals an' they're chust waitin' through there for us. Jonah's gonna let the Englishman go first."

"You're too kind."

They crept towards the darkened corridor, straining their ears for any sign of the cave's inhabitants. They heard nothing but the pounding of their own hearts and moved away from the light into the all-enveloping blackness.

Forrester edged forward, fumbling against the damp stone for support. Each tentative step further into the dark was fraught with the terrors of the unseen and unknown. Jonah followed close behind, so close that Forrester could feel the hunchback's short, anxious breaths on his naked back. Unlike the underwater tunnel, the passageway did not follow a straight line. It turned and snaked its way through the timeless rock of the island, deeper into its cold dark depths and further away from the warmth and light of the sun.

"Look ahead," Jonah croaked, his rough hand gripping Forrester's shoulder. "There's more light!"

His words were unnecessary as Forrester could not have failed to see the ethereal blue glow that illuminated the large chamber into which they stumbled.

The cavern was vast, far larger than any of the others they had passed through that day. Perfectly circular in shape and with a tall, domed ceiling, it was clear to both men that it was not a natural rock formation but something carved out of the heart of the island over a long period of time. Every inch of the rock walls was decorated with intricate engravings inlaid with silver and mother-of-pearl. The engravings seemed to represent a pictorial history of the creatures who inhabited the caves, though many of the images were far too complex to make sense of them. The sheer scale of the undertaking took Forrester's breath away as he reflected that what they looked upon was the culmination of hundreds of generations of work.

The tunnel from which they emerged was at the top of a number of tiered levels, hewn from the solid rock. The tiers followed the circumference of the whole chamber and led down to a polished stone floor on which stood a large crystal which gleamed with the same phosphorescent light as the rocks in the pool. The crystal was unlike any Jonah or Forrester had seen before, standing at least ten feet high and so perfectly symmetrical it was hard to believe that it was not some kind of expertly cut piece of glass. The blue light that emanated from the crystal flooded with chamber with light and fell on the dozen or so figures gathered around its base.

"He wanted tae find the nest o' the Blue Men," Jonah whispered. "Jonah reckons he's lookin' at it. Now what daes the Englishman have planned? Somethin' about these boys tells Jonah he cannae chust stroll on down there an' join 'em before their big blue stone."

Though he spoke in hushed tones, the acoustic properties of

the chamber were such that his voice carried to the creatures stood on the polished stone. A howl went up from them and they turned to glare at the intruders in their lair.

Jonah brandished the marlin spike he had brought from the boat but Forrester grabbed his arm and held it firmly.

"Use your head, man," he hissed. "Start waving that thing around and they'll rip us limb from limb. There's too many of them to fight."

The creatures moved from the floor of the chamber and scrambled onto the first few tiers. Their movements were graceful and unhurried, as though they did not consider the possibility of their prey attempting to flee. The creatures drew closer and Forrester was able to get his first clear look at them.

They were uniformly tall and thin. Well muscled and hairless, their bodies seemed perfectly designed for a life of swimming. Their arms were slightly longer than a man's and Forrester noted the webbed skin between their fingers. All were cursed with the same hideous facial features: wide yellow eyes, gaping mouth filled with small pointed teeth and the small nasal slits that substituted a nose.

The females were slightly shorter than the males and appeared less densely muscled. This difference in size, however, did not prevent them from advancing alongside their mates and they seemed no less intent on attacking their unwelcome visitors.

"What daes he suggest?" Jonah whispered, trembling as the first of the beasts clambered onto the tier beneath them.

"I need you to speak for me," Forrester spoke hurriedly. "Translate everything I say into Gaelic, every word. And for heaven's sake, don't get it wrong – our lives depend on it."

"Aye, no pressure then," Jonah groaned.

Chapter 16

Forrester swallowed drily and began to speak, his attention focused on what he said and not the horrors scrambling towards them.

"Men of the Minch! I come here not as an enemy but with the open hand of friendship. I cannot speak your tongue but I ask you to be patient with me and my companion. Hear what we have to say before you attack those who wish to help you!"

Jonah translated his words quickly and the creatures froze as they heard the hunchback speak.

"He's got their attention now, man," Jonah whispered. "Now tell 'em tae piss off."

The creatures gazed expectantly at Forrester and he continued.

"I have no doubt that you have swum these waters for many years and have had little contact with the men of the long island. They tended the land and left you to deep waters. Your paths have seldom crossed and you are therefore unaware of the true nature of man. Now that men have discovered the riches of the deep and the means by which to harvest them, they stray into your waters and cast their broad nets for the fish that you see as your own.

"Though I am not from the long island, I understand men well. For all his talk of God and human kindness, man is cruel and dishonest. Though he talks of charity, man is no more likely to show benevolence to others as he is to cut off his own two feet. I am here to tell you that you have been deceived by the man who calls himself Murdo Macleod."

At the mention of the name, a number of the creatures hissed and blinked their large yellow eyes in recognition. One pushed his way to the front of the throng and clambered up onto the ledge on which Forrester and Jonah stood. It was a male, taller than the rest, his wiry body covered with a lifetime's worth of scars. He moved with the haughty bearing and confidence of a leader and the manner in which the other creatures deferred to him confirmed this.

Towering above them, the creature prodded a long finger into the ribs of the trembling hunchback and spoke in Gaelic with sibilant tones.

"This good-lookin' cove calls himself Finn Meic Uilleim," Jonah said, unable to pull his gaze away from the hideous face of the creature. "He's askin' what ye ken o' Macleod."

"Murdo Macleod has lied to you, just as he lies to his fellow men in Stornoway."

The creature shook his head and hissed a response.

"Macleod is a good man. He keeps the other fishing boats away from our waters," Jonah translated.

"He has tricked you," Forrester answered. "You allow his boats to fish the Stream of Blue Men and no others. Macleod grows richer and richer with every month that passes and soon he will own most if not all of the fleet in Stornoway. What then, Finn Meic Uilleam? How will your precious fish be protected if they are caught in Macleod's nets?"

The creature's yellow eyes glared at Forrester as Jonah translated and Forrester returned the unwavering gaze. When Jonah had finished, the creature stood silent for a moment before snarling and turning his back.

"Jonah disnae think he believes ye," the hunchback muttered and placed a hand on Forrester's shoulder.

Forrester shook off Jonah's hand and took a step towards the creature.

"A man like Murdo Macleod cares for nothing but his own gain. He will keep taking more and more and his greed will not be satisfied until every fish in your waters lies in his nets. The fishing season does not start in earnest until next month but already his boats are taking thousands of fish from your waters. He has boasted to me of a further twenty five boats coming across the Minch to help him in the summer season. Surely you will not allow this fleet to fish your waters in his name? What is to stop him bringing fifty boats next season or a hundred the next?

"The men of Stornoway feared these waters before Macleod began fishing them. Why should you fear the boats of the long island but not those of Murdo Macleod!"

"Daen't listen tae him!" a voice thundered in the darkness.

Forrester spun on his heel and saw the three figures stood in the mouth of the tunnel. Murdo Macleod stepped forward into the chamber, followed closely by Jack Macphail and Rowan Campbell. Macphail's blackened eyes glittered with malevolent glee when he saw Forrester. Campbell and Macphail each brandished a long filleting knife whilst Macleod was in possession of Forrester's own revolver.

"This is no' yer business, ye daft English bastard," Macleod roared. "What good d'ye think ye can dae?"

Forrester didn't flinch as Macleod levelled the gun at his face. Though he doubted the fisherman had much experience with firearms other than hunting rifles, he did not wish to give him the opportunity to learn. Nobody moved. Campbell and Macphail remained within the mouth of the tunnel, wary of setting foot in the domain of the creatures. The creatures themselves watched the proceedings with interest, their rasping breaths echoing in the lofty cavern.

The silence bore down upon them. Forrester knew the Webley was a heavy gun but Macleod's hand remained steady. Macleod's dark eyes remained fixed upon him, his lips curled into a permanent sneer. Forrester watched Macleod thumb the hammer back on the pistol, waiting for the right opportunity to attempt to retrieve his weapon.

"If he disnae mind, Jonah will be leavin' the now," Jonah said, his voice breaking the tension.

"Ye're no' goin' anywhere, Crotach," Macleod snarled, his finger tightening around the Webley's sensitive trigger.

"How long did you think you could fool them for?" Forrester asked. "Did you think you could ply them with smuggled whisky and hope they wouldn't notice a fleet of your boats fishing their waters?"

"Ye've been nothin' but a nuisance since ye arrived, Mister Forrester. Always askin' questions... same as that blasted young fool Ali Mackinnon. Ye understand that I didnae want tae kill the wee lad, but we couldnae trust him tae keep his mouth shut."

"You'll hang for this."

Macleod shook his head solemnly.

"No, Mister Forrester. The only crime the Sheriff could find me guilty of is no' payin' duty on a few dozen bottles o' whisky - an' given that he's gey fond o' a dram, I doubt he'd find me guilty."

Macleod took a step closer and braced himself to fire. Seizing his opportunity, Forrester leaped forward and barrelled into the big man. The gun went off as they tumbled to the ground, the bullet ricocheting off the roof of the cavern and the shot echoing in the darkness like a tremendous thunderclap. The noise of gunshot unnerved the creatures and they scattered to the refuge of the shadows, leaving the two men to exchange savage blows as they wrestled for the weapon.

The knife glittered in Rowan Campbell's hand as he moved to assist Macleod but Jonah lunged at him with the marlin spike he still held. Campbell stepped aside from the tip of the spike and slashed Jonah across the back of the neck. The momentum of his lunge carried Jonah further forward than he had anticipated and he stumbled to the hard stone floor. Campbell raised the knife to slash once more when a second shot rang out and the stray bullet struck him in the centre of his chest, throwing him backwards.

With one hand Forrester clawed at Macleod's face, the other frantically grasping for the pistol. Feeling teeth bite down hard on his fingers, Forrester yelled with pain and slammed his head forward into Macleod's face. Over and over they rolled, the ferocity of their blows increasing until Macleod struck out with his elbow and wrenched the pistol free from Forrester.

Macleod rolled away from his stunned adversary and sprang to his feet. He spat blood and smiled through split lips as he took aim. As he squeezed the trigger the marlin spike thrown by Jonah struck him in the shoulder and the shot went wide.

The bullet shattered the crystal which had hitherto lit the cavern and an unfathomable darkness smothered the pale blue light. At once a chorus of cries went up from the creatures, their terrible shrieks joined in unison. Though he could not understand the words, Forrester knew their meaning. The creatures that had watched the strange altercation between the two men were no longer content to stand passively. Their sacred light source destroyed, the beasts meant to punish the humans who had so arrogantly set foot in their lair.

The blackness was absolute but Forrester could hear the creatures moving about and their furious hissing. Something moved close to him and he flinched when a hand grabbed his arm.

"They're no' happy, man," Jonah whispered. "Can he walk? Jonah reckons it's time tae leave."

Forrester took hold of the hand that was offered to him and was hauled to his feet. Jonah led the way through the darkness and Forrester dazedly shuffled alongside him, his arm clamped firmly around his companion's deformed shoulder.

As they stumbled into the mouth of the tunnel they heard a frenzied scrabbling followed by a shriek of agony that was unmistakeably human.

"Sounds like they got hold o' Macleod," Jonah muttered as they staggered onwards in the gloom.

Macleod's anguished cries followed them through the darkness of the tunnel and out into the dim blue light of the smaller chamber. They stood at the edge of the pool and gazed into the water illuminated by the strange phosphorescent rocks beneath the surface.

"Is he fit tae swim? Jonah disnae think he can drag him through."

"I can swim," Forrester replied, "but you should go first."

Jonah did not need telling a second time and jumped straight into the water, taking a deep breath before paddling beneath the surface into the submerged tunnel that was their only means of escape. Forrester prepared himself to dive but froze as he felt the sharp end of a knife press into the small of his back.

"Bi samhach!" Macphail spat, bringing the knife around so that the blade rested against Forrester's throat.

Shuffling steps could be heard from the inky blackness of the passageway and Forrester could feel Macphail tremble as the creatures drew closer.

"You hear them?" Forrester muttered. "We can't stay here, they'll tear us limb from limb as soon as they find us. Our only chance is to swim!"

"Bi samhach!" Macphail repeated, his voice cracking with terror.

Forrester grabbed the arm that encircled his neck and pulled, ducking his head as low as possible. Macphail was lifted off his feet and the two men plunged into the icy cold water. The reckless throw took Macphail by surprise and as he floundered in the pool Forrester kicked himself free and swam towards the underwater tunnel.

Forrester entered the mouth of the tunnel, his hands grabbing the rough surfaces to heave himself through the narrow channel cut in the solid rock. A hand latched around his ankle and he felt the keen blade of Macphail's knife slice into his thigh. He looked behind and lashed out with his free leg, his foot striking Macphail's face with enough force to loosen the grip and propel himself further forward. He paddled frantically, drawing on his last reserves of strength as he struggled out of the confines of the tunnel and burst to the surface of the water, gasping for breath.

Jonah had already clambered into the boat and was hauling in the anchor. Seeing Forrester, he offered his hand and hauled the exhausted man out of the freezing water.

"What kept him?" Jonah asked as Forrester slumped against the stern of the boat.

"There's no time. Get us out of here!"

As Jonah grabbed the oars another figure emerged from the depths and clung to the gunwales. Macphail said nothing as he tried to pull himself into the boat but his wide eyes looked imploringly at Forrester for assistance. Jonah plunged the oars into the water and the boat began to move.

Forrester watched Macphail's desperate attempts to climb aboard but did nothing to help him. His attention was fixed on the sleek grey forms which had risen from the dark water and swam around the cave. They moved gracefully in the water, their broad strokes causing barely a ripple as they circled the boat.

When Macphail spotted the approaching shapes he redoubled his efforts to pull himself out of the water and sobbed hysterically each time he felt one of the things brush past his legs. A sudden jolt caused the boat to lurch wildly and Macphail cried out in anguish. His cries were quickly silenced as he was dragged beneath the surface.

The water beneath the boat seethed and churned as the creatures swarmed the helpless man. Forrester scrambled over to Jonah and grabbed one of the oars as a dark red stain began to spread across the water. Together, they rowed the boat out of the oppressive gloom of the cave and into the open air.

They raised the sail as quickly as they were able and watched the canvas billow in the wind. Jonah said nothing as he gripped the tiller, his eyes fixed on the open sea before them.

"What if they follow us?" Forrester asked. "We've no chance in the water against those things."

Jonah tossed Forrester his pistol.

"Jonah stumbled across it in the dark an' thought it might be of use. If one o' those bastards comes close tae the boat he can shoot the beastie."

"And when we run out of bullets?"

"Dinnae bother Jonah with details! Can he no' see he's busy steerin' the boat?"

The wind was strong and the small boat skipped across the waves. Several grey shapes followed the boat at a distance and Forrester kept his gun trained on them. Though the creatures did not come close to the boat they kept up their pursuit for the best part of a mile and the men in the boat remained uncomfortably aware of their presence long after the towering cliffs of the islands had faded into the distance.

"What are they doing?" Forrester muttered. "Why aren't they attacking us?"

"They're chust makin' sure we're leavin'," Jonah replied nervously. "Looks like they believed his story but I dinnae imagine we'd be welcomed back."

"That's fine with me, Jonah. I've no intention of going back there. Take us home, I feel the need for a stiff drink."

Chapter 17

Forrester slept through most of the next day. He did not dream and did not stir once from his deep slumber. When he finally clawed his way back to consciousness, he found himself in strange surroundings and sat up quickly. A sharp pain rang through his skull as he struck his head on the low wooden ceiling of the box bed in which he lay. Rubbing his aching brow, he pulled himself out of the bed and stretched.

Looking around the room, he recognised it as the main room in the Morrison's blackhouse. However, the customary tidiness of the house had been replaced with the chaotic clutter of a household in turmoil. The fine china that had decorated the dresser was now wrapped in paper and packed into crates whilst the less valuable items had been discarded in a darkened corner. Caitlin Morrison knelt on the floor and carefully sorted through a small collection of silverware. Looking up from her task, she flashed Forrester the same dazzling smile as he had received from her daughter.

"Ye're a fine sleeper, Mister Forrester," she chuckled. "Angus was worried ye might never waken."

"I apologise if I have been of any inconvenience to you."

"Och, nothin' o' the sort," she said, waving a dismissive hand. "The bed's been empty since Effie moved tae the town an' has been wantin' a warm body tae fill it."

"You're packing your things," Forrester stated, gesturing towards the crates.

"Aye, we're flittin'," she sighed. "The factor raised the rent again an' there's nae money left in this land."

"Where will you move? The mainland?"

Caitlin shook her head and a nervous laugh escaped her lips.

"A wee bit further than that. We'll be crossin' the other water next week."

"The Atlantic?" Forrester gasped. "You're going to America?"

"Canada first, but Angus has a few old friends who flitted tae New York. We're hopin' tae spend Christmas wi' them."

"And Effie?" Forrester asked. "Is she going with you or will she be staying here?"

Caitlin avoided his gaze and busied herself with the silverware before her. "Perhaps ye'd best talk wi' her about it. There's a ceilidh on tonight. Ye'll see her there, if ye're feelin' well enough."

"Right as rain," Forrester puffed out his chest and put on a brave face in spite of the fact that the numerous cuts and bruises on his body left him feeling older than ever before.

Forrester watched Caitlin sort through the small heap of silver cutlery. She took each piece in turn, polished it and then wrapped it in a scrap of cloth from a pile by her side. She hummed a few notes of a tune and a tear rolled down her cheek before she caught herself.

"I'm a wee daftie, I know," she sniffed. "There's me tellin' poor Angus for years that we should be flittin' an' him refusin' an' when I finally get my way I cannae stop myself greetin'."

"Are you sad to be leaving the island?"

"I've ne'er been further than Glasgow. The very thought o' crossin' an ocean an' travellin' tae the other side o' the world is pure terrifyin'."

"How does Angus feel?"

"He's sad tae be leavin' but there's nae future for us here an' he kens that fine. We've barely a penny left from buyin' the tickets but he's confident tae find work when we arrive."

"So the ceilidh tonight is some kind of farewell party?"

"Aye," Caitlin managed a smile as she pushed herself to her feet. "An' if ye're plannin' tae join in the drinkin' we'd best be fillin' your stomach wi' some food. Come, let me fix ye some porridge."

In no time Forrester was sat on the bench, a bowl of steaming oats in his hands. Caitlin watched him eat but did not trouble him with conversation. When he placed his empty bowl beside him, she snatched it up and refilled it.

"Angus won't go tae a ceilidh without his oats," she commented. "He says the whisky goes straight through him without at least two bowls of porridge."

"It's delicious."

Caitlin watched him eat for a few more mouthfuls before she turned to the sideboard and began rummaging through one of the smallest drawers.

"I almost forgot," she said, "Calum Mackinnon brought this letter over. He'd been lookin' all over town tae find ye. His cousin Boyd sent it on from Glasgow."

Forrester took a look at handwriting on the envelope and groaned.

"Who sent it?" Caitlin asked. "Someone you know?"

"It's from Chief Inspector Pardoe, my superior on the force."

"Are ye no' gonna open it tae see what he wants?"

"I've a fair idea what it will say," Forrester muttered as he ripped open the envelope and unfolded the letter.

Caitlin watched with interest as Forrester's eyes scanned the letter. His expression grew sterner as he read and by the time he had finished reading his brow was furrowed and his lips had twisted into a sneer.

"The damn fool," he snarled and tossed the letter onto the smouldering peats in the centre of the room. In seconds, the paper had been reduced to ash.

"What did he say?"

"Nothing of consequence." Forrester rose to his feet. "It doesn't matter now, nothing does."

***

The tigh ceilidh was situated at the foot of Beinn na Saighde. Similar in shape to a blackhouse but significantly longer, the tigh ceilidh was only used for community events such as those of the evening. There was a gathering of locals outside who warmed themselves by a bonfire and greeted the merry-makers with enthusiasm. Forrester stepped through the low doorway into the smoky interior of the house and was taken aback by the number of people crowded inside. Through the fog of smoke Forrester could distinguish a band at the far side of the room. They comprised of an aged fiddler, a bodhrán drummer and Jonah with his accordion. The noise they made was terrible but mercifully could not be heard over the roar of voices united in song.

A hand pressed into the small of Forrester's back and he turned to find Effie stood behind him.

"I brought ye a dram," she said, handing him a glass of whisky.

Forrester thanked her and took a mouthful of the spirit. Seconds later he was spluttering and gasping for breath.

"Careful now!" she laughed. "Ye shouldnae be knockin' that back so fast. Not unless ye're wantin' tae end up on your backside before the night is through."

"It just went down the wrong way, that's all," Forrester croaked, still feeling the potent spirit burning the back of his throat.

"Oh aye," she smirked. "Of course it did."

He raised the glass again and took a more restrained sip. She raised her eyebrows in a gesture of mock surprise and took him by his free hand.

"Dance wi' me?"

"I'm English."

"What's that got tae dae wi' dancin'?"

"A true Englishman has no sense of rhythm. We don't dance because we can't."

"Ye're talkin' shite," she slapped his hand playfully.

"Nothing of the sort," he answered, squeezing her arm and trying to lead her away from the other dancers.

Effie pulled him back towards her and took the glass of whisky from his hand. She upended the glass and drained the contents in one gulp. With a wink, she handed the empty glass back to him before turning away to join the other dancers.

Forrester watched with envious eyes as a handsome young man in a kilt swept Effie across the floor. The band struck up a frenetic reel and the revellers voiced their approval with a chorus of whoops and cheers. Effie threw back her head and appeared to shriek with glee though her cries were lost in the noises of the crowd. Forrester suppressed his rising jealousy and tried to engage in the spirit of proceedings, tapping his feet in time to the beat of the drum.

Caitlin spotted him and pushed her way through the throng to stand by his side. "Ye're no' dancin'?" she asked, refilling his empty glass from the large bottle she clutched protectively.

"I'm none too light on my feet," he replied. "Besides which, I don't know the steps."

"Och, that shouldnae bother ye, chust follow what the others dae."

With that she gave him a forceful shove and thrust him into the ring of dancers. No sooner did he realise what was happening had his hands been taken by the women on either side of him and he began to move with the rest of the circle. The dance was complicated, full of claps and turns, curtseys and bows. He lost count of the number of times he stumbled over his own feet and felt ungainly when partnered with the young women who skipped lightly into his arms. Round and round the circle spun, the dance further complicated by the fact that the participants were required to swap partners with each rotation. Each of the girls who grasped hold of him appeared sympathetic to his predicament and were happy to take the lead.

Another trade of dance partners brought Effie into his arms and her eyes glittered with delight as she swung him around. He leaned in close to make his voice heard over the frantic music but before he could utter a word she had pecked him on the cheek and flew off into the arms of another man.

Effie's place was taken by her mother who snorted with glee and joined him in the final steps of the dance.

"I told ye it was no' difficult," she said, joining in the riotous applause that followed the close of the tune.

"It was very energetic," he panted, secretly exhilarated by the experience.

"Ye did well. I think ye're deservin' another drink."

The evening continued along similar lines. A dram of whisky led to dancing and the dance was always rewarded with another drink. Caitlin and Angus introduced Forrester to a seemingly endless procession of their friends and extended family, most of whom appeared to be called Donald. The men shook his hand vigorously or embraced him with a rib-crushing bear-hug. When he could take no more, Forrester excused himself and slipped outside into the cool night air.

Having walked a short distance away from the tigh ceilidh, he sat himself on the edge of a peat bank and lit a cigarette. The night was clear and thousands of stars glittered in the firmament above. The silhouette of a woman slipped out of the open doorway and made her way across the croft to where he sat. Effie seated herself next to him and took his hand in hers. They sat that way for some time before either of them broke the silence.

"Are ye enjoyin' yerself, Edmund?" she asked.

"Very much so."

"Why are ye sittin' alone in the dark?"

"I just needed a few moments by myself, to reflect on things."

"Mother told me about the letter Calum brought over. Is it something serious?"

Forrester flicked the end of his cigarette away and watched the dying embers fade into the darkness. When no answer came, she did not press him but squeezed his hand encouragingly.

"Are ye upset wi' me, Edmund?"

"Your mother tells me they're going overseas," he said solemnly. "Are you going with them?"

"No' now," she whispered, "dinnae be doin' this tonight."

"Were you planning on telling me before the ship sailed?" he continued. "Did you not think that I might have wanted to know?"

"Edmund, what d'ye want of me?"

"I want you," he uttered, taking her by the shoulders and gazing deep into her eyes. "I want us to be together."

"That's no' gonna happen," she pulled away from him, "I'm leavin'."

"I'll come with you."

She shook her head and wiped the tears from her eyes.

"What about your job an' your life in England?"

"To hell with them," he spat. "I had no life to speak of back there and by the sounds of things I won't have a job for much longer at any rate."

"What d'ye mean?"

"That letter, the one Calum brought over, it was from Pardoe, my superior. He was demanding my instant return on threat of dismissal."

"Ye must go," she implored.

"The letter was sent days ago," he shrugged. "Even if I were to set off tomorrow morning it would be the best part of a week before I could get back to London and it'd be too late by then anyway. I imagine they're clearing my desk already."

Effie rose to her feet and brushed the dirt off the back of her dress with her hands. Turning away from him, she gazed at the stars and wrapped her arms around herself.

"I told ye that I wanted stability. A man who wouldnae run off an' leave me. I took a beatin' from Macleod an' his crew for ye an' what did ye dae? Ye strode off an' near got yourself killed. When I saw ye at the quayside all cut up an' delirious I thought I was gonna lose ye. I nursed ye back tae health an' kept ye hidden from Murdo Macleod. How did ye repay me? Ye ran off an' left me again tae go finish yer stupid fight.

"I begged ye, Edmund, I cried till my eyes were raw an' I begged ye no' tae go. But ye still did. I cannae live wi' a man who'll do that."

He stood behind her and wrapped her small frame in his

arms.

"I'll never do that to you again," he whispered into her ear, "I promise."

"Ye will," she wept. "Men like you cannae help it. Ye're born tae it."

"What can I do?" he asked.

She turned in his arms so that she faced him and took his face in her hands.

"Nothin'," she said, the tears in her eyes sparkling in the moonlight. "Ye must understand that it's for the best. I'm goin' tae America an' I don't want ye tae come."

Their lips came together and they kissed for the last time before she slipped away and left him alone in the darkness.

***

The huge steamship dwarfed the other vessels in the harbour and drew the attention of the whole town. The quayside was crowded with people, all of whom cheered those who stood on the deck of the ship. Handkerchiefs were waved, horns were blown and endearments to friends and loved ones were shouted above the roar of the crowd. There was such a gathering of people on the quay that Forrester doubted he could have elbowed his way to the front in order to wave farewell to the Morrison family. Standing back from the crowd, he leaned against a wall and searched the figures on deck for any sign of Effie.

The ship's two large funnels belched smoke into the sky which mingled with the dark grey clouds hanging ominously over the town. Reaching into a pocket, Forrester removed his handkerchief. He contemplated waving it at the ship, but only momentarily. His natural sense of restraint got the better of him and he decided that it would be put to better use by wiping his nose.

"Jonah thought he'd find the English here," a familiar voice spoke.

Forrester's gaze broke away from the deck of the ship and he turned to see the hunchback stood by his side. Jonah grinned crookedly at him and offered him a drink from a hip-flask. Forrester declined the offer but returned a half-hearted smile.

"Your music at the ceilidh last week," Forrester said. "It wasn't as bad as it could have been."

"It's a shame Jonah cannae say the same for the Englishman's dancing."

They laughed at the joke but quickly lapsed into an uncomfortable silence. Jonah could see that Forrester's gaze was fixed on the huge ship that was preparing to leave the harbour.

"The blone is leavin'?" Jonah asked.

"She is. I can't see her on deck."

"The Englishman did what he had tae." Jonah placed a consolatory hand on Forrester's shoulder. "Jonah cannae think of another man that'd dae more for a strange town."

"Any word from Macleod's crew?"

"Not a peep," Jonah snorted. "We'll no' see them again. They'll have fled the island faster than rats leavin' a sinkin' ship."

"And those things, the Blue Men... What of them?"

"They'll no' be goin' anywhere. The Minch has always scared the fishermen, an' Jonah plans tae tell all who'll listen tae steer well clear o' the Sound o' Shiant. Those waters belong tae them, and Jonah's no' gonna argue."

"Very well." Forrester nodded thoughtfully. "Then by my reckoning, I'm finished here."

"Daes the Englishman have a plan?"

"I'll head back down to England. I'll probably spend a few nights in Glasgow before catching the train to London. I'm in no particular hurry."

"And the gyurl? Is he no' goin' tae follow her?"

"To America?" He shook his head. "That's another world, I couldn't possibly."

A bitter wind blew across the harbour. Jonah sighed and buttoned up his woollen jacket against the cold. Having clasped Forrester's hands in farewell, the hunchback began to walk away with his peculiar stride. He had gone no more than ten paces when he stopped and turned to face his friend.

"He can dae whatever he wishes," Jonah called, "but the Englishman would have tae be a fool if he would do all that fightin' for a place he owed nothin' an' then not fight for somethin' he loves."

Forrester opened his mouth to answer but his words were drowned out by a long, low blast of the ship's horn. He shrugged his shoulders at the interruption and joined the rest of the town as they waved to the departing vessel.

Author's Notes

I first visited the Isle of Lewis in October 2006. I stayed for a week and it rained constantly. Though I vowed never to return, my wife and I moved here in 2009 to be close to her parents. Living and working here has given me a great love for the rugged beauty of the island and its people. I have tried, as much as possible to use real locations in this novel but I hope I will be forgiven for any liberties I have taken for the sake of storytelling.

Music has always played an important part of the life of the islands and to capture this, I included a number of folk songs in the novel. The herring girls and Murdo Macleod sing traditional Gaelic waulking songs that can be found on the internet, whilst Jonah the hunchback sings songs that are collected in Francis J. Child's "The English and Scottish Popular Ballads".

The stories of the Blue Men of the Minch are hundreds of years old and are a sadly neglected part of the rich folklore of the islands. Unrelated to kelpies or mermaids, the Blue Men are the Western Isles own unique cryptozoological beasties.

Those wishing to learn more about the Shiant Isles should read Adam Nicolson's wonderful book "Sea Room: An Island Life". It was in this book that I discovered details of the Campbell family who lived on the island from 1862 until 1901.

The Prologue details the wreck of the Norwegian schooner, the Zarna. Captain Lorentzen and his crew did indeed all perish in the Sound of Shiant but as far as I know, the Blue Men had nothing to do with it.

Special thanks must go to Pat Black for help with editing

and all the good folks at Booksquawk for their ongoing support. Extra special thanks must go to Chris Cowdrill for his sterling work on the book's cover design.

This novel is dedicated to my wife who first introduced me to the wet, windswept island that I currently call home. Without her patience, understanding and enthusiasm this book would not have been possible.

Hereward L.M. Proops

May 2012